A HEARTH ROMANCE

Romance Along the Bayou

Sallie Lee Bell

ZONDERVAN
PUBLISHING HOUSE
OF THE ZONDERVAN CORPORATION | GRAND RAPIDS, MICHIGAN 49506

The town of Lamare, the people, and the incidents in this story are entirely fictional.

Any similarity of names, places, or incidents is coincidence and not intentional.

ROMANCE ALONG THE BAYOU

First Zondervan Books edition 1974
Ninth printing 1981

Library of Congress Catalog Card No. 64-22833
ISBN 0-310-21022-4

Printed in the United States of America

Romance Along the Bayou

ZONDERVAN HEARTH BOOKS 

Available from your Christian Bookseller

Book Number

Hearth Romances

2	*The Deepening Stream*	Francena Arnold
3	*Fruit for Tomorrow*	Francena Arnold
4	*Light in My Window*	Francena Arnold
5	*The Barrier*	Sallie Lee Bell
6	*By Strange Paths*	Sallie Lee Bell
7	*The Last Surrender*	Sallie Lee Bell
9	*Romance Along the Bayou*	Sallie Lee Bell
10	*The Scar*	Sallie Lee Bell
11	*The Substitute*	Sallie Lee Bell
12	*Through Golden Meadows*	Sallie Lee Bell
13	*Until the Day Break*	Sallie Lee Bell
16	*This Side of Tomorrow*	Ruth Livingston Hill
17	*Give Me Thy Vineyard*	Guy Howard
19	*Judith*	N. I. Saloff-Astakhoff
20	*Trumpets in the Morning*	Lon Woodrum
21	*Light From the Hill*	Sallie Lee Bell
22	*The Bond Slave*	Sallie Lee Bell
27	*The Queen's Jest*	Sallie Lee Bell
28	*Young Man, Young Man*	Eda Stertz
30	*'Til Night Is Gone*	Phyllis Primmer

Hearth Classics

29	*Right On With Love*	Lon Woodrum
31	*The Warm Summer*	Craig Massey

Hearth Mysteries

8	*The Long Search*	Sallie Lee Bell
14	*Candle of the Wicked*	Elizabeth Brown

Sebastian Thrillers

23	*Code Name Sebastian*	James L. Johnson
24	*The Nine Lives of Alphonse*	James L. Johnson
25	*A Handful of Dominoes*	James L. Johnson
26	*A Piece of the Moon is Missing*	James L. Johnson

To

Betty Lee Bell

Romance Along the Bayou

CHAPTER 1

LORAMIE HERNDON sat on the wide porch of the lovely colonial home and drifted idly back and forth in the wide swing. There was a dissatisfied look in her hazel eyes and her full red lips drooped in discontent. She was bored. She hated this little Louisiana town, for she saw none of its beauty — the winding bayous that led through the marsh lands beyond the town, the beautiful moss-draped oaks that had been there for centuries, nor did she appreciate the picturesqueness of the townspeople who were descended from the French Canadians. They had been deported here from their northern home during the French and Indian War.

They were just "Cajuns" to her and she looked down on them as an inferior people, ignorant and superstitious, with whom she had no desire to be friends.

Though this temporary home was beautiful and furnished with priceless antiques, she despised it, because it lacked many of the modern conveniences to which she was accustomed in her luxurious home in New Orleans.

Her father, Frank Herndon, had accepted the position of conservation commissioner until a successor to the deceased commissioner could be appointed. This had necessitated their moving to the town of Lamare, so that he could be near to his duties. He was not only anxious to fulfill his job with the utmost conscientiousness, but he also had political ambitions. He desired the friendship of these people, for he knew that he would need their vote if he should run for the office he hoped to win. He was wealthy, but he had ambitions to become a force in politics.

Mrs. Herndon was a frail woman who lived the life of a social butterfly and Loramie was following in her mother's footsteps. They were both bored by the life in Lamare, but Mrs. Herndon made frequent trips to the city to enjoy her social engagements and Loramie sometimes went with her. She felt that life here was causing her to be left out of her social group, because she could no longer be a part of their everyday life and fun.

This afternoon she was alone and had nothing to do that interested her. She had read until her eyes were tired. She was thinking of her friends in the city and that they were sure to be having a good time. She wished that she had gone to the city with her mother.

As she swung back and forth, wishing that the months would soon pass so she could return to their home in New Orleans, she heard a car approaching and coming into the driveway. It was her father's car. As he drew nearer she saw that there was a man with him. She flicked her half smoked cigaret into the nearby flowerbed. She had been smoking constantly while sitting there. Her mother, who had some old-fashioned ideas about women smoking, often reproved her. However, she gave the excuse that so many smokers give, that smoking quieted her nerves, though she failed to understand that smoking did just the opposite and only made her more nervous.

As the car stopped and the two men got out, Loramie noticed that the man with her father was young, not over thirty perhaps, and that he was quite good looking. The bored look in her eyes gave way to an expectant look and her lassitude vanished as her lips parted in anticipation.

As the men mounted the steps, Loramie gave her father

a smile and waited for the introduction.

"Mr. Darnell, meet my daughter, Loramie," her father said as they stopped before the swing.

Mr. Darnell bowed and gave her a smile as he acknowledged the introduction.

Loramie returned the smile with a ravishing one as she murmured a greeting.

"Mr. Darnell is to be our house guest for a while," her father explained. "He is here to see about obtaining trapping rights in this parish."

"We shall do our best to make your visit a pleasant one," Loramie said with another smile. "You'll find this town a pretty dull place to exist in."

"With such a charming hostess, I'm sure that I won't have to look to the town to make my stay a pleasant one," he told her.

She knew that the compliment was not in good taste, but she ignored that trifle. He was good looking and he evidently thought her attractive. She was sure that he would prove an interesting diversion in her bored existance.

"I'll have the maid show you to your room while I go and interview the cook about dinner," she said as she left them and went inside.

Morton Darnell looked after her as she disappeared and there was no doubt in his host's mind that Darnell found his daughter attractive. Darnell's words confirmed his belief.

"You have a beautiful daughter," he commented as they followed the maid to the second floor."

"Thank you," Herndon replied. "Of course I think so, but then I'm rather prejudiced. She is all I have and both her mother and I have spoiled her, I'm afraid. I'm sorry that my wife is in town, but she'll be here before long. She will be glad to have you as our guest. Life is rather dull for the women here and you will prove a most welcome diversion for them."

"Thanks for the compliment."

By the time dinner was ready, Mrs. Herndon had returned, and the meal was a more lively one than the family had known for quite some time. Morton Darnell proved to be an entertaining conversationalist and Loramie, roused from her boredom, was sparkling and quick with repartee.

She noticed Darnell's eyes admiring her. She was used to being admired, for she was quite beautiful, but, after such a long, dull period, his admiring glances thrilled her more than she would otherwise have been.

Following dinner, they went into the living room for a while, then her parents left them together and Loramie led him outside in the cool darkness to the swing.

"This is my favorite place to go when there is nothing else to do but sit and wait for time to pass," she remarked as they sat down together and rocked gently to and fro.

"Is life really so dull here?" he asked.

"It is for me. I miss the gay life in the city. There was always something interesting to do, if only a swimming party at the club, or a gabfest with the girls."

She asked him where he lived and he told her something of his life in the north, of the home and the family he had left behind, parents and a sister and younger brother and how he missed them even in the short time he had been away from them.

"Then you didn't leave a wife behind?" she asked.

"No, there is no wife," he told her. "I wish there was, but somehow I've never found just the right one. Or should I say that those whom I might have cared for, didn't care for me."

"Then I shall feel free to do my best to make you enjoy your stay with us."

"Would the fact that I had a wife have made any difference?" he asked with a smile and a lift of his brows.

"It surely would," she replied with a little laugh. "While I was trying to make you have a pleasant time, I might have been treading upon dangerous ground with a married man."

"I understand, and I admire you for your attitude and for your frankness," he told her.

The tone of his voice and the look in his eyes which she

saw in the dim light from the hall, told her that he was interested in her in a very special way. She knew the look, for she had seen it before.

She was pleased to have it so. It would be a welcome relief from a dull life. This new friendship might prove to be quite interesting. Perhaps it might prove to be more than friendship. Time would tell.

CHAPTER 2

THE NEXT MORNING Herndon and Darnell left early and they didn't return until time for the evening meal. Loramie wondered why Darnell was here and what his business was. She had forgotten that her father had mentioned the business that had brought him. While they were talking the evening before, they had not had time to discuss such topics as business. There had been more interesting things to talk about. That evening she did ask. Her father answered her question.

"Mr. Darnell is here representing a big fur firm in the north. His company has plans to extend their business by using nutria fur in their trade. The local trappers are only interested in trapping muskrats and nutrias are only a bother to them. I'm trying to help him get the trapping rights to this section. We don't think there will be any trouble with the trappers, though this will bring in outsiders."

"But won't the native trappers feel that their rights are being interfered with?" Loramie asked.

"I'm sure that when they are convinced that they won't be hurt by the new trapping rights, they won't make trouble. The new traps can be put out right along with their traps. Mr.

Darnell's company is only interested in nutria, not in muskrat furs."

His answer satisfied Loramie, for she wasn't really interested in the trappers or their rights. If she had noticed Darnell's face during this explanation, she might have wondered at his expression, but neither she nor her father observed it.

She knew nothing about trapping rights and her only interest in the affair was the fact that this kept her father here in Lamare until the end of the year. And that couldn't come too soon for her.

Later that evening she and Darnell again sat out in the swing and talked until bedtime.

"I'm sorry to have to leave so soon after having met you," he said, "but I shall have to be gone for a little while in the morning. I was expecting to have a very dull and lonesome time while I was down here, but I've been so pleasantly surprised by meeting you. I'm sure that I shall enjoy my stay here to the utmost if you will only give me a small part of your time."

She uttered a little laugh. "Time is my greatest possession while I'm in this place. Having you as our guest will be a pleasure. I shall look forward to your return."

"It will be only for a few days," he told her. "I was dreading to have to return here, but now I shall look forward to returning."

"You're a great flatterer," she said, "but I like it just the same. It makes me think of a story a friend told me about her grandmother. The old lady was buying some beauty preparation. Her skin was like a wrinkled prune but the sales person kept telling her what a lovely skin she had. When they left the store, the grandmother turned to her granddaughter and said, 'I knew it wasn't true, but it made me feel good, just the same.' "

"But what I say isn't mere flattery. It's the truth," he said seriously. "This may sound silly to you and you may think I'm saying idle words, but the moment I met you, I was sure that you would be someone very special in my life. Am I foolish to hope that what I feel is not objectionable to you?"

"Oh, this is so sudden, Mr. Darnell!" she said with pretended amazement.

They both laughed. They were in the mood when they could laugh at nothing in particular. He felt her charm and the attraction of her beauty in a way that he had never experienced before and she couldn't help but be a little thrilled over his obvious earnestness and sincerity. She had never had quite this direct approach from any of her admirers before. She valued it more because she knew that this man was older and that he had had experience before this with other girls. Besides he was good looking and charming in spite of his sometimes rather crude flatteries.

"It is sudden for me and I'm sure it is for you," he said seriously, "but I want you to know that I am serious. I've never said anything like this to any other girl so soon after meeting her, but then I've never felt like this before. Please don't be angry with me or think me presumptuous for letting you know how I feel."

"I'm not angry, if you are sincere," she replied as seriously.

"Will you be equally honest and sincere with me?" he asked.

"Do you doubt my honesty, sir?" she asked with mock indignation.

"No, I don't, but I know how many girls react when they know that a fellow is interested in them. I don't believe you're like them, but I want to be sure that you won't lead me on, as many of them would."

"Lead you on, sir? How can I lead you on when I don't know where you intend to go?" There was a playful note in her voice, but he ignored it.

"I think you know, but perhaps I've said too much. Just be kind to me when I return. I'll be so impatient to get back."

"I'll try to be," she conceded.

During the few days while he was away, Loramie thought of what had passsed between them. She wondered if he was really in earnest or if he took her for a gullible youngster, since he was so much older than she was. She found him quite interesting at any rate and she couldn't decide whether it was his personal good looks or his too evident interest in her that made her question his sincerity.

She had enough vanity to know that with her red gold hair, her hazel eyes and lips that seemed made for kisses, she was beautiful and attractive to the opposite sex, but she also knew that he had known girls who were as pretty and were perhaps more sophisticated than she. There was the possibility that he might trying to use her for what help he hoped to receive from her father.

She had become more interested in the trappers since Darnell's arrival than she had ever been. She wondered just what kind of a firm Darnell represented and how long it would take him to obtain the rights he wanted. She wondered if what he hoped to obtain, which would bring new men into this territory, would upset these poor men when their territory was invaded by strangers. These people were very clannish and loyal to each other and she had heard stories of killings which had taken place when they thought their lands had been invaded by other native trappers. She hoped there wouldn't be trouble, for if there was, her father's hopes to win the friendship of these people and their vote for him if he should run for office in the next election would be shattered.

She decided that she would ride out as far as she could and take a look at what lay beyond the road that led through a part of that section.

The road ran along the bayou and in the distance she could see young cranes standing on their long thin legs, dipping into the sluggish stream for their food. Occasionally one would fly away, looking like a miniature plane, with wings spread wide and long slim legs stretched out far behind. There were many other birds in this sanctuary. They flitted through the moss-hung trees and twittered or sang in their clear throated tones. There were little wrens that warbled melodiously, and mocking birds that darted here and there, driving the smaller birds away while they uttered harsh warning cries.

She saw a beautiful aigrette resting upon a branch nearby and she admired the lovely feathers which were used on women's hats until a law was passed forbidding their use. The hunters did a cruel thing to these lovely feathered creatures, for they killed them in their nesting season. The mother bird would not leave her eggs or her young so she was taken and the feathers torn from her throat and breast and she was left to die while the little birds slowly starved to death.

This bird had evidently finished raising her young, for she sat quietly upon a branch, oblivious of the noise of the other birds.

She rode on through the tree-covered area and finally came out to an open field which was surrounded by trees, through which the bayou wound its slow way.

In the distance she saw the watchtower which had recently been erected in order to keep illegal trapping and hunting out of this restricted area, a sanctuary set apart by the government. She had heard her father say that there was a stranger there now, acting as temporary watchman while the regular watchman was away. She wasn't interested enough to remember the man's name when her father was talking about him.

She stopped the car and sat there for a while, looking across the bayou to the land that lay beyond, wondering what lay in those shaded areas. Presently she saw someone climbing down the steps from the watchtower and walk to a canoe tied at a landing. She watched him with interested eyes, for he was striding across the grass covered area with long graceful strides.

She started the car and rode slowly toward him as he approached the canoe. As she drew nearer, he looked around at the sound of the car and saw her. After a moment of surprise, he waved to her in the unconventional way of the friendly people in this "Cajun" country. Then he gave her a second glance of undisguised admiration.

She saw the look and she smiled. She was used to that look, but it pleased her nevertheless as she observed it in the eyes of this stranger. He was strikingly handsome, with dark hair that tossed to and fro in the breeze, deep expressive eyes and a firm chin that spoke of character as well as a strong will.

"May I give you a lift, if you're going to town?" she asked impulsively.

She was surprised at herself for having spoken and she regretted it because she was afraid that he might not understand her motive.

"Thanks a lot," he said, "but if I took you up on your offer, I would have to walk back. Don't tempt me."

"You won't have to walk back," she told him. "If you won't be too long in town, I'll be glad to bring you back. I have some shopping to do and I've only ridden out here to kill time. I have lots of that."

"I was on my way to the post office," he said. "If you really mean that I won't be a bother, it would be wonderful to get a ride to town. It's like a ray of sunshine on a dark day to be able to talk to someone like you after being so far from home and alone so much of the time."

"It won't be a bother at all," she assured him, "and I'm as lonely as you are even though I have my parents with me."

"Thank you so much," he said as he got in the car, and she drove slowly toward town.

"You must be a stranger here," she remarked.

"Yes. I live in Virginia. I had hopes of becoming a successful lawyer, but a sudden illness brought on more trouble and my doctor ordered me to get out in the sun and just rest until I was able to get back to work again."

"Climbing that watchtower can't be restful," she remarked.

"I couldn't have done that six months ago," he told her. "My father had a friend down here and he asked him to let me come down and stay with him until I got strong enough to come home. He thought that this warm southern sun and air would help me to get well faster than where we lived. This friend had the bright idea of letting me take this position as watchman to relieve the one who was on a long sick leave. So when I grew stronger, I got the job and here I am, just a man on the watchtower."

"That's quite a story," she said when he had finished.

"And far too long," he apologized, "but you asked for it." Again his engaging smile flashed across his lips.

"I'm glad I did," she told him, "and I've enjoyed hearing it. I wondered how you could be satisfied with a position like this. That is, after I saw you," she added as she looked into his expressive eyes.

"If that is a compliment, thank you. I wouldn't choose this as my life's work, but this has been a great help to me physically. I just hope that I haven't kept someone else from taking the job who might have needed it more than I did. I've thanked the Lord many times for the opportunity it gave me to regain my health."

A little flicker of surprise shone in her eyes at the mention of the Lord, and in such a way. She seldom heard the name mentioned except in church, which she didn't attend too often.

"I haven't introduced myself," he said. "I'm William Fenner. My friends call me Bill."

"Will you count me among your friends?" she asked with a roguish lilt in her voice and a smile upon her lips.

"At the top of the list," he told her in the same light vein.

"I'm Loramie Herndon," she said. "My parents sometimes call me Lorrie, but I hate that nickname. My mother used to call me that when I was naughty because she knew I hated it."

"Loramie Herndon, what a lovely name!" He paused while his eyes scanned her face and said things which he dared not utter. "Then you are the daughter of Mr. Herndon, the conservation commissioner."

"Yes. Dad took the position for the unexpired term until someone else could be appointed. I'm sure you must find life here as dull as I do. I can scarcely wait until we can get back to the old life at home."

"Life is rather lonely at times," he confessed. "But there are so many interesting things here and so many interesting people that I can't say that life is dull. I've made some friends who have found a place in my heart and whom I shall never forget. Then when I'm not scanning the area for possible law breakers, I can snatch time for reading. As soon as my car arrives, I can get to town more often and not have to paddle that old canoe. Dad wouldn't send it down until he had word from the doctor that I was strong enough to be turned loose again. That sounds like I'm a reckless driver, but that's not what I mean. If I had that car, he was afraid that I wouldn't take enough exercise and that's what I've been needing."

"Then perhaps sometime you can drop in on me for a little visit," she suggested hopefully.

"Your father might not welcome the visit of a watch-tower guard," he said. "I'm not in the same social class as your other friends just now."

"I choose my own friends," she said with a little toss of her head. "And social position has nothing to do with it."

"Then I shall count it a privilege to come to see you."

They chatted until they reached the town and she dropped him off at the post office. He told her something of his life at college and incidents of his studies at law school, of his father's hopes for him to enter politics and then the sudden blast of their hopes when his sudden illness had come.

"I'm sure that this was the leading of the Lord," he remarked. "I didn't like the idea of politics, even though I feel that this country needs the services of dedicated men who put God and honor above greed and graft, but I don't feel that this is my calling."

She was again surprised by his second reference to God in the way he mentioned Him. She wondered just what kind of a person he was. He was quite different from the men she had known. He interested her more because he was different.

"But even if you don't care to enter politics, I suppose you'll continue your law practice when you get back home," she remarked.

"I'm not quite sure what I shall do," he replied. "I've had a lot of time to think and to take stock of my life, and I'm just waiting to know what the Lord would want me to do. It's a great opportunity, I realize, to defend someone who has been falsely accused. I might be able to help some young fellow who has started on the wrong road, but if I practice law, I would have to defend some criminals whom I know to be guilty and that wouldn't be easy for me to do. It wouldn't be easy for me to try to save someone who deserved to pay for some crime that he had committed."

"I never thought of it that way," she said, still more surprised and mystified. "I thought that when a lawyer took a case, he did everything in his power to prove his client innocent, even though he knew him to be guilty."

"So he does, but I just couldn't do that, for it would entail living a lie with my own conscience. If the court appointed me as a lawyer to someone who didn't have the money to pay for one, I'd have to take the case. This isn't often done, but it would present a problem that I wouldn't want to have to cope with."

"Afraid?" she teased.

"No," and he smiled. "Just having to decide whether to be true to my convictions or to live a lie in order to save a criminal whom I know to be guilty."

CHAPTER 3

WHEN SHE HAD let Bill out at the post office, she went into a shop nearby and began to look around, for she had told him that she was going shopping. She looked with a certain attitude of disdain at the meager display of merchandise, but she was greeted in such a friendly manner by the clerk that she felt she should buy something. She bought several articles and began a conversation with the person who had waited on her.

While they were talking, a young girl came in and stood there staring at her. When Loramie turned and looked at the girl, she noticed such a look of hatred in the girl's eyes and in her every expression, that Loramie felt a sudden shiver of fear. She shook off the feeling at once, told the clerk good-by and walked toward the door.

As she went outside, she heard the few words that passed between the girl and the clerk.

"Who ees she? What ees her name?" the girl asked.

"I don't know, Yvonne," the lady said. "She is a stranger here."

"I hate her! I could keel her!" the girl cried.

"Don't talk like that," the lady said. "You don't even

know her. Run along and forget such terrible thoughts or I shall tell your father."

Loramie didn't stop to hear more, but hurried toward the post office. Bill was standing in the doorway waiting for her.

By the time they were on their way and Bill was talking, she had momentarily forgotten the girl and her threatening attitude.

Bill's eyes were shining for he had been reading his mail. He held an open letter in his hand.

"You must have had good news," she observed as he folded the letter and put it back in the envelope.

"I have. Mighty good news. Judy is back from the hospital and the doctor says she will be all right. I've been so worried about her. She had broken several bones in a bad fall and was in pretty serious condition."

"Who is Judy?" Loramie asked.

"She's my kid sister and a regular little tomboy. She's always getting into some kind of a scrape and has had so many accidents that it's getting to be a habit. She's the baby of the family, born years after the rest of us, and we all spoil her. I'm glad that I'll be going home before very long, so that I can be with them all again." A faraway, yearning look crept into his eyes.

She felt a sense of relief to know just who Judy was and she wondered why she hated to hear him say that he would be leaving soon. What difference should it make to her whether he went away or stayed? She would probably never see him again unless he kept his promise to come to see her. This he might never do.

She asked him about his family and was intensely interested in his whimsical accounts of their life, more interested than she would have thought possible. His strange ideas about God, and the casual, yet reverent way he mentioned Him, as if He were a real Person intimately connected with his life, interested her.

She wanted to ask him about this, but she dared not, for she didn't really know just how to ask what she wanted to know. From what he had said and the way he mentioned

Him, she felt that he had some new religious belief, different from anything she had encountered in her brief and sketchy church attendance.

There was no Bible in her home, or if there was, she had never seen one, and there never was a mention of anything pertaining to religion or belief in God. The only time worship was mentioned was a criticism of the length of a sermon or an argument about what the preacher had said about trying to live a better life by helping others and sharing what one had with those who had less.

"Sounds like socialism to me," her father had commented one day after such a message. "I wonder if he is leaning toward communism."

When they returned to the place where Bill had to leave her, he extended his hand and gave her a lingering handclasp while his eyes gave her a message that stirred her heart.

"You can't possibly know what this meeting with you and your kindness has meant to me," he said.

His voice was mellow and she knew that she could never forget those husky, vibrant tones, for they did something to her rapidly beating heart.

"It has meant a bright interlude in a lonely existence," he said.

"I've enjoyed this as much as you have," she told him. "I, too, have not only been lonely but bored beyond words."

"I shall look forward to accepting your offer to let me come and see you," he told her. "If that offer still holds good, I shall come whenever you're not too busy to see me."

"I'm never too busy," she informed him, "and I shall be glad to see you whenever you care to come."

"Thanks again for such a pleasant time," and he gave her a warm smile, then turned and went with springing stride over the grassy space to the tower.

She sat there watching him as he went toward the tower and her thoughts were confused. She had never met anyone quite like him and there was a magnetic force about him that attracted her. At least she told herself that this was the cause of her interest. He wasn't any more handsome than some of her former boy friends, but his outlook on life and his very manner of conversation were so different. The boys she knew were so full of nonsense, even though they had good educations. Their silly chatter often bored her. Perhaps that was why she had never been really interested in any of them. She had found Darnell interesting and he entertained her with conversation that she enjoyed. For that reason she had looked forward to his return and hoped to have a pleasant time with him while he was in her home. Now that she had met Bill, she had lost her enthusiasm and the anticipation of his return. In retrospect, in comparison with Bill, he didn't seem interesting at all and she felt that she wouldn't care how long he remained absent.

As she rode toward home, she remembered the girl who had looked so threateningly at her in the store, the girl called Yvonne. Why did that girl seem to hate her when she had never seen her before and why did she say that she would like to kill her?

Perhaps it was only because she was a stranger. She knew that these people were for the most part friendly toward everyone, still some of the older ones continued to retain an animosity toward the English. They still held the bitter hatred that had been handed down to them from their ancestors. They had been cruelly deported from their homelands to this land by the English who were then their enemies.

The girl had a strange wild beauty, with black eyes that shone like two candles of hatred, and straight black hair that hung in disorder about her thin face. She could have been only sixteen or seventeen at the most. It was terrible for her to have such violent hatred for someone she had never seen before.

When she reached home she found her mother already there. She was sitting on the porch looking idly over the lovely garden.

She waved to Loramie as she drove into the driveway.

"I wondered where you were, honey," she said as Loramie mounted the steps and sat down beside her. "You should have gone to town with me. I met some of your friends at Mrs. Stone's garden party and they asked about you and said they missed you. You would have enjoyed being there."

"I would have been bored to death at that garden party," Loramie replied. "Mrs. Stone always gives such dreary affairs. Who wants to sit around at a garden party and chatter when they could be somewhere else dancing and having fun?"

"Anything's better than being buried out here," her mother remarked. "I'll be glad when we see the last of this place."

"I'll agree with you about that," Loramie told her, but in her heart she felt that she would hate to leave if that time came before Bill Fenner left.

She shook herself mentally and rebuked herself for being so silly. She was acting like a kid again, letting her heart flutter at the look of a young man's eyes and the firm clasp of his hand. She was ashamed to admit it even to herself.

"I forgot to tell you," her mother said. "There's a letter for you on the table in the hall. Your father got it yesterday and forgot to take it out of his pocket."

Loramie went inside and got the letter. She knew from the postmark that it was from Morton Darnell. She tore it open and read it.

"Who is it from?" her mother asked.

"It's from Mr. Darnell. He says that he'll be delayed longer than he thought. I suppose that Dad already knows this."

She didn't tell her mother what else the letter said. He told her once more what it had meant to him to know her and that he was looking forward to seeing her again. This new friendship with her meant more to him than he dare say now. He hinted in carefully worded phrases that he hoped it would ripen into something more than just friendship and that she was the only girl he had ever known who had awakened such a desire in him.

His words left her cold. She had heard the same thing, though not put in such well worded phrases, from many others. Perhaps a day or so ago she would have been pleased with what he said and would have looked forward to at least a little flirtation with him, but now she didn't even have the desire.

It was strange, she thought, how a few hours could so change a person's feelings and a person's interest.

CHAPTER 4

LORAMIE WAITED EXPECTANTLY for Bill to pay the visit he had seemed so anxious to make, but as time passed and he didn't come, she decided that he wasn't interested and that she'd better forget him.

As she sat in the swing late one evening, she heard the sound of a car, and to her surprise, she saw it enter the driveway. When it stopped, Bill stepped out and the change in him surprised her. He was immaculately dressed in a dark suit and his hair that had been so unruly lay in a wavy mass over his brow.

She rose to meet him as he mounted the steps.

"This is a surprise," she exclaimed. "Your canoe has turned into a car. Quite a miracle."

She was a little bit disappointed to see that he now had a car. She wouldn't be able to give him any more lifts to town.

"Yes. At last I'm allowed to drive again and Dad shipped my car down. It's such a relief to have it. If I hadn't gotten it, I wouldn't have been able to come to see you and I'd hate that."

"I thought perhaps you had forgotten all about me and

your promise to come to see me." She could have bitten her tongue for letting that silly remark escape her.

"How could I forget?" he exclaimed. "It would have been almost impossible for me to come after hours, in the canoe, so when I knew my car was coming, I waited impatiently for it to arrive. It just came today. Now perhaps I can return your kindness in giving me a lift. Perhaps I can take you somewhere in my car and then perhaps you can come out to the tower and let me show you over my territory through the field glass."

"That would be interesting," she said, trying to keep the enthusiasm out of her voice.

While they were talking, Mrs. Herndon came out and joined them. She was curious to know who Loramie was talking to, for it was so unusual for her to have company, especially at this hour.

Bill stood up as she approached and Loramie rose also and introduced them.

"Mr. Fenner is in charge of the watchtower on the sanctuary," Loramie explained.

Mrs. Herndon couldn't conceal her surprise and Loramie hastened to explain how she had met him.

"I met him by accident the other day when you were in town and I drove out along the road leading through the marshes."

"Miss Herndon was kind enough to give me a lift to the post office. She saved me from a long ride in my canoe," Bill told her.

"Won't you sit down and join us, Mother?" Loramie invited, though she hoped her mother would refuse the invitation.

"No, I'll leave you two young people to yourselves," she said, much to Loramie's relief. "It was nice meeting you, Mr. Fenner," she said to Bill. Her voice held a chill politeness.

She was surprised and perturbed that Loramie should have met such a person and in such an unconventional manner. She was provoked with Loramie for accepting this stranger as if he was in their social set. Loramie surely must be bored to have stooped to this.

Loramie was enjoying herself so much that it surprised her. Bill was very interesting and entertaining and though his eyes in the faint light on the porch told her things that she wanted to see in them, he didn't stoop to banal compliments. She appreciated this and realized the innate refinement of the man. It was in contrast to Darnell's clumsy attempts to flatter her. She was glad that neither her father nor Darnell was there. If Darnell had been there, it would have been embarrassing for her and possibly for Bill.

"May I come again soon?" Bill asked as he prepared to leave. The time had passed so pleasantly that Loramie hadn't realized how late it was.

"Why certainly," she assured him. "I've enjoyed your visit immensely. It's been so much better than reading myself to sleep or else looking at some of the silly things they show on TV."

"Even if I'm a poor substitute for reading or TV, I'm glad to be of service," he said jokingly.

"I didn't mean it that way," she said with a little embarrassed laugh. "But anyway, do come again."

"Will you come out to my workshop and let me show you what I see through my telescope?" he asked.

"Yes, I'll come. I'm sure that it will be interesting." She was glad of an excuse to see him again soon.

When she went inside she found her mother still up and there was fire in her eyes.

"What keeps you up so late, Mommy dear?" she asked sweetly, ignoring the look in those eyes so like her own. "You should be in bed getting your beauty sleep."

"That's where you should have been long ago," her mother retorted. "Do you know what time it is?"

"I haven't the least idea," Loramie answered with a shrug of her shoulders. "When a person has company, it isn't polite to consult one's watch."

"I'm sure your father won't be pleased with your friendship with this man," her mother said acidly. "Neither am I. How on earth did you condescend to strike up an acquaintance with him and invite him to call?"

"I didn't strike up an acquaintance," Loramie told her, though she knew this wasn't the truth, considering the way she had met him. "He told you that I gave him a lift and he asked me if he could call, so I told him he could. I was so bored I would welcome a visit from anyone."

"Then you had better go into town and stay at home with the servants and mingle with your friends until we can join you," her mother advised.

"I'm staying here, Mother," Loramie said firmly. "Please don't suggest that again, and don't get any idea of shipping me off just because I've found a friend who is entertaining. He is not just a common laborer, as you seem to think. I'm not going to leave here until we all do."

"We'll see what your father says when I tell him about this strange fellow whom you've found so interesting."

"It doesn't matter what he says," Loramie retorted angrily. "You and Dad had just as well realize that I'm no longer a child and that I have a right to choose my friends, so long as they're decent people. You know me well enough to know that I wouldn't do anything to disgrace you. And this young man is everything that I could desire as a friend. If you would take time to listen and believe, perhaps you would know that he has just as good social standing as we have."

"If he does, he wouldn't be here serving as a menial watchman in a marsh," her mother informed her angrily also. "And I don't want to listen to your explanation or your excuses. Go to bed. That's where both of us should have been long ago."

Loramie left her without her usual goodnight kiss. She lay upon her bed wide-eyed and thinking. She didn't know whether it was a perverse spirit of rebellion or whether she was genuinely interested in Bill Fenner. At any rate, she was determined to continue the friendship, that had been started so unconventionally, with the young men who had become the object of contention between her mother and herself.

Morton Darnell returned unexpectedly the next afternoon. He drove up in an expensive car and greeted Loramie effusively.

"I can't begin to tell you how glad I am to be near you again," he said with a look in his eyes that she had seen there before, but which now left her cold.

"Won't you say you're glad to see me?" he asked when she had given him a perfunctory greeting.

"I am," she said, though there was no enthusiasm in her voice. "I hope your visit was successful."

"It was — most successful," he told her. "For example, see the car that has been placed at my disposal. And there is a beauty of a launch being sent down for my use. It will take me to every part of the territory where the car can't go. I hope that you will consent to go with me at times to look over the land. The launch has a nice little cabin and a cover that will protect your lovely skin from the sun."

"I shall look forward to going with you," she told him.

"Just a break from the monotony?" he asked playfully.

"Not just that," she denied with a smile. "I shall enjoy being with you and with Dad when he can go."

"I shall have to be satisfied with that," he said regretfully, "though I was hoping for more enthusiasm from you."

"Be satisfied with small blessings and perhaps greater ones will come later," she advised jokingly.

"I just hope the greater blessings will come soon," he replied.

Mrs. Herndon came out just then and greeted him warmly.

"Loramie will be so happy to have you here again," she gurgled. "We have all been looking for your return."

She cast a glance at Loramie which Loramie understood. She said nothing.

CHAPTER 5

WHILE DARNELL was waiting for his launch to arrive, he drove out frequently toward the swamp land. He asked Loramie to go with him occasionally and she was glad of the opportunity to get away from home and not to have to drive alone so often.

She asked him about his plans to get the trapping rights, but he was persistently vague in his answers. She wasn't particularly interested in his business affairs, so she didn't notice his evasions. She did ask him one question, however.

"How long will you be here looking over this territory?"

"I'm not sure how long it will take before I choose the exact location that we wish to occupy. I want to be sure that we can use the territory with profit to our firm. I understand that the nutria is a menace to the trappers who are only interested in trapping muskrats, but we can use their fur in many ways. Why do you ask? Are you anxious to be rid of me?" and he gave her a playful smile.

"Of course not. I was just wondering how much looking around you would have to do before you applied for exclusive trapping rights to the section you want to occupy."

"I don't care how long it takes me, as long as I won't be a bother to you," he said. "Just to be near you will compensate for whatever delay there may be. I should stay at the hotel in the city, but it would not only be most inconvenient, but rather lonesome. I do appreciate your father's insistence that I stay here. While I'm here, I can look forward to spending some time with you when you have nothing else to do."

"I'm sure that Mother and Dad are glad to have you stay with us," she told him. "And as for my having anything else to do, I never do have anything in particular. I'm just living for the time when I can be home again with my friends. Mother goes into town often to play cards or to attend some tiresome tea, but I don't care for cards or teas. I never go unless there is something special."

"Would you go with me and have dinner and then go to some show?" he asked.

"I'd be glad to," she told him.

They were driving out to the place where Loramie had first met Bill and she was looking for a sight of him as they approached the watchtower.

"That fellow must be pretty hard up to take a job like that," Darnell remarked as he stopped the car for a moment and they both looked at the tower in the blazing sun. "He must have a lonely time of it."

Loramie didn't reply, for she saw Bill getting into the canoe. He paddled away from them toward the deeper part of the swamp land.

"I wonder what he's up to now," Darnell said as they saw him disappear around a bend in the stream.

"He must be going to inspect some part of the territory to see that there are no hunters poaching out of season."

She was wondering why Bill hadn't returned as he had asked to do.

"I suppose he'll still keep his job, even if you get the trapping rights," she remarked.

"I suppose so, for he's in charge of the government owned sanctuary and has nothing to do with the trappers or their rights. I just hope that he won't take it on himself to be a nuisance. If he does, I'll take steps to see that he doesn't interfere."

"Let's hope that that won't happen," she said. "I would hate to see any trouble on account of your desire to get the trapping rights."

She knew even now, that if trouble did come, she would be on Bill's side.

A few evenings later she and Darnell went in to New Orleans. They had a delicious meal which Loramie enjoyed and then they went to a current movie and returned rather late. Loramie noticed that her mother wasn't waiting up for their return and that she didn't even ask her the next morning what time it was when they came in. She knew that her mother was quite pleased with the attention that Darnell was paying her.

The next morning after the men had left, Mrs. Herndon told Loramie that Bill had called the evening before, just after they had left.

"I told him that you had gone to town with the man to whom you would soon be engaged," her mother informed her with a note of triumph in her voice.

"Why did you tell him that when you know it isn't true!" Loramie exclaimed heatedly.

"I thought it was good for him to think that, for then he would keep away. He wouldn't be having any hopes as far as you're concerned."

"He didn't have any hopes, so far as I know," Loramie retorted. "All he wanted was to be friends, for he was lonely down here, though he has made many friends among the natives. He's a fine young man and he has a right to come here if he wants to, but now you've spoiled everything. He won't be coming any more, for I know you must have been rude to him."

"That will be just fine," her mother stated. "And I don't like you calling me rude. I only told him what I hoped would soon be the truth."

"You did a cruel and selfish thing, Mother, and I don't

like it,'' Lorraine said in an aggrieved voice. ''If you think you're going to throw me at Mr. Darnell, you're mistaken. He's very nice, but I'm sure that I could never love him, so if you're hoping to have him for a son-in-law, just get that hope out of your mind.''

''Time will tell,'' her mother insisted. ''Mr. Darnell is a very good-looking man and I think he's very attractive. I'm sure he's in love with you and perhaps when you know him better, you'll see what a happy life he could give you. Just don't be hasty in discouraging him, dear.''

With that she left Loramie.

Loramie was so angry with her mother for the way she had treated Bill that she had very little to say to her until her mother had left for the city. Her mother wisely let her pout, for she thought she had gotten rid of someone who might have proved an annoyance, since Loramie had showed so much interest in him.

As soon as her mother had left for town, she drove out to the watchtower. She wanted to see Bill and try to set him straight about what her mother had told him.

She saw him climbing the tower stairs and she got out of her car and went to the tower.

''Hello, up there!'' she called when she had reached the foot of the stairs. ''Do you allow visitors at this time of the day?''

He looked down at her and gave her a smile.

''Some visitors are always welcome, no matter what time of day it is. Come on up. Sorry I didn't see you sooner or I would have come down to greet you.''

She mounted the steps and was soon beside him at the top. She looked about her with interest and she saw what a neat room it was. There was a desk and a couple of chairs at one side and on the other side near the big window there was a telescope. She noticed that there was a book lying open on the top of the desk. She wondered what he had been reading.

''You said that I might come sometime and visit you and see the world from your telescope. I came at the first opportunity, though I was looking for another visit from you.''

"I did come to see you," he told her, "but your mother gave me the brush-off. She said that you had gone to town with the man to whom you'd soon be engaged."

"Mother was using her imagination," she replied. "Dad has a friend staying at the house and he has been nice to me, because, I suppose, he feels that as a guest he should be." She knew that this was not the truth, but she didn't mind a little "white lie," if it met her need. "I'm sorry I missed you. I would have enjoyed your visit more than I did that silly picture."

"I feel flattered," he said with a whimsical smile, "but I'm afraid that I won't be welcome at your home any more. Your mother made that quite obvious. I could sense that by her coolness and the tone of her voice. I'm sorry, because I looked forward to spending more time with you. Meeting you has meant so much to me."

His voice became low and tender and his eyes said more than his words.

"Thank you for saying that, because I can return the compliment," and a smile flitted across her lips. Then seriously, "I want us to continue to be friends, even though Mother might not be cordial if you should come to see me. We need each other. I'm as lonely as you are and I want to help you to be less lonely. So, if you won't come to see me, I shall have to come to see you," she added playfully.

"Nothing could please me more, though I had hoped we could go to the city and have a meal together sometime."

"We can still do that, if that is what you want us to do," she asserted. "I'm not a child and I think I have a right to choose my friends as long as they are respectable people and I do think you come under that category."

"I hope I do. At least I try to be," and his smile flashed again.

"Then any time you're free, we can go, either to dinner and a show, or else just to dinner. It would be fun either way."

"I'm afraid it will have to be just dinner," he said, "for I don't go to shows."

"I'm sorry I suggested it," she said after her brief start of surprise. She felt embarrassed, for she knew that she had practically asked him to take her to a show. "May I ask what you do to pass the time when you're at home?"

"I found, when I stopped going to movies, that there were so many more worthwhile things to take up my time that I wouldn't have had time to go to them if I had still wanted to."

"Life must be pretty dull for you," she remarked, still feeling her surprise.

"No. Life is more interesting and happier now than it has ever been," he contradicted.

She felt nervous and she searched in her purse for her cigaret case and realized that she had left it in the car. She craved a smoke.

"I forgot my cigaret case. I left it in the car. Do you happen to have one? I'll pay you back," she added with a little nervous laugh.

"Sorry, but I don't smoke," he said.

"How strange," she exclaimed, feeling embarrassed again and more nervous. "I thought practically everyone smoked. Is it on account of your health?"

"No. My health had nothing to do with it. I used to smoke. I was practically a chain smoker, but when I accepted Christ as my Saviour, I gave it up. I knew that smoking was not what a Christian should do. I confess that at first it was quite a struggle, but the Lord helped me to gain the victory over it."

"What do you mean by being a Christian?" she asked. "Aren't we all Christians, if we're not heathen?"

A smile flitted across his lips. "No, we're not really Christian unless we have accepted Christ as Saviour, until we have confessed to God that we're sinners and have asked Him to forgive us and to save us for Christ's sake, He who shed His blood for our redemption."

"What kind of religion is that? I never heard it put that way before," she said, surprised and wondering.

"Not a *kind* of religion," he explained. "It is just

believing God's Word and accepting salvation that He so freely offers to everyone who believes His Word and receives it."

He crossed to his desk and held up the open book he had left lying there.

"It's faith in this Word that keeps me going and believing its promises that keeps me happy, even while I'm lonely and away from those I love. It tells me what the Lord Jesus did for my salvation and it also tells me that one day the Lord Jesus is coming back again to take His redeemed ones out of this old world to meet Him in the air and to be with Him forever."

"That's the Bible, I suppose," she remarked. The person she was now looking at seemed a different person from the Bill she had known such a short time.

"Yes, don't you have one?" he asked, somewhat surprised.

"No, I don't, and if there is one in my home, I've never seen it." She felt embarrassed and somehow rebuked as she admitted this.

"Will you let me tell you more about what is in it, sometime?" he asked.

"Yes, I will," she said slowly.

He was wise enough not to continue the conversation upon that subject any longer.

"Come over and take a look through the telescope," he suggested. "There is a beautiful view from some angles. In the early morning, the sound of the different birds singing brings a sweet music that you can't hear in the towns where people live."

He set the telescope for her and helped her to turn it in every direction. She was amazed at the clarity with which she could see in the distance.

"Now I understand how you can keep such a sharp eye on the game preserve," she commented. "It would be easy to spot poachers."

"Fortunately I haven't had to charge anyone for that so far," he said. "I don't think any of these people in this vicinity would dare to come here except when the hunting season is on, for they know the law and they do try to abide by it. I know how poor many of them are and I'm sure that many times they must be tempted to steal in and get some forbidden game. I would hate to have them do that, for I would have to have them punished and I know what a hard struggle many of them have to keep on living."

"You're very tender hearted," she remarked with a warm light in her eyes, "and I respect you for it. So few ever think of the other person."

"I appreciate that," he said gravely.

When it was time for her to go she told him that when he was ready, she would go with him on that promised date.

"What will your mother say?" he asked. "I don't want to make any trouble."

"I shall tell her and if she wants to be angry, I'll be sorry, but I shall go anyway. I can't let her rule my life that way. I think I can make her understand that we're just friends."

"I'm sure she wouldn't want us to be more than that, or even just friends," he said with a wry smile. "She feels that a tower watcher is no fit person for her daughter to be interested in, if only as a friend."

"If she would let me tell her that your family is quite prominent in your home town and that you're a lawyer with influential connections, she might change her mind about you."

"Please don't tell her that," he urged. "If I can't be accepted for myself, I wouldn't want what my family is and what my connections are to make any difference to anyone."

"You don't know Mother," she said with a little laugh. "Please leave it to me, for I do want your friendship, no matter what she may think about you."

"That's what I want too," he assured her with a smile.

CHAPTER 6

LORAMIE HATED to admit to herself that she was eager to have Bill keep his promise to take her out to dinner. On this afternoon, both her mother and father were in the city and Darnell had left upon one of his trips, so she was alone. Her mother, as usual, wanted Loramie to go with her, but she refused to go. She was hoping that Bill would phone and she didn't want to miss his call.

He did phone late in the afternoon and she was relieved that she wouldn't have to face her mother and her wrath when she told her that she was going to town with Bill. Though she knew that she would eventually have to have it out with her mother, she dreaded the ordeal and was glad to know that it would be postponed.

When he came and they drove to town, she enjoyed not only the ride, but his pleasant conversation and she was happy just to be with him. They dined in the French quarter, in a restaurant where she had eaten many times, but never before, she admitted to herself, under such pleasant circumstances.

While they discussed the menu the waiter stood by expectantly. When they had decided upon their order, the waiter asked them what they would have to drink. Loramie waited silently for Bill to give his answer. She was used to having some small drink, a cocktail or something, before a meal in a restaurant. It wasn't that she particularly cared for liquor, but among her crowd, it was the expected thing to do whenever they were out for a meal together.

"Nothing but coffee for me," Bill said and turned to her.

"The same for me," she echoed.

While they ate and talked, Loramie was thinking about the conversation and the incident about the Bible. She wanted to talk about that again, but she didn't know how to approach the subject.

Following the discussion with Bill about the Bible she had asked her mother if she had a Bible.

"I think so," her mother told her, somewhat surprised at the question. "It's around home somewhere, but I have no idea where it is."

"Don't you ever read it?" Loramie persisted.

"No, I don't. I never seemed to have time after I was married and I've almost forgotten where I put it when we moved into our present home. Why this sudden interest in the Bible?"

"I was just wondering," Loramie evaded. "The last time I was at church, the preacher said that every home should have a Bible where it could be easily reached when the pastor came to visit. He told it as if it was a joke. I wondered what would happen if he should visit us and ask for a Bible."

"There's little chance of that," Mrs. Herndon said rather bitterly. "Since your father refused to contribute to one of his pet projects, he's given us the cold shoulder. That's why we so seldom go to church."

"I suppose you used to read it when you were a girl," Loramie remarked.

"Yes, your grandmother saw to that," and a little smile hovered upon her lips at the memory. "Mother was a wonderful Christian but she tried to force her children to follow in her footsteps. If she had been less commanding and more gentle and persuasive, perhaps we would have followed her, but the way she handled us, made us want to pull the other way. We had to read a chapter a day, but when I married, I was too busy to bother, so the Bible she gave me was put away and forgotten."

"I'd love to see it," Loramie commented. "It must have some wonderful truths in it."

"What makes you so suddenly interested in the Bible?" her mother repeated. "Is Mr. Darnell interested in it?"

"Oh, no!" Loramie exclaimed. "I doubt if he even knows the existence of a Bible, unless he's seen it on the pulpit of some church."

"Then it must be that young man who seems to have made such an impression on you," her mother surmised. "If he has, he's been putting on an act just to make you believe that he's someone when he's nothing."

"Oh Mother, you're impossible!" Loramie cried, impatient and provoked. "I'm sorry I ever brought up the subject. Just skip it. Why should Mr. Fenner pretend to be something he isn't, when he doesn't have the slightest idea what my religious belief is?"

She remembered this conversation as she and Bill sat there. He was both amusing and entertaining and she was enjoying the evening to the fullest. Most of the conversation of the boys she had known was just silly chatter and she had often been bored by it. But there was never a dull moment in this evening's outing. Bill's conversation was serious as well as amusing as he told her some interesting facts about his work, the creatures he was protecting and some of their interesting habits.

"I'm sorry that I can't offer to take you to a show," he remarked as they finished their meal.

"I won't miss it," she assured him. "I've had such a pleasant time and it has been far more interesting than some dull picture. I can go to a show anytime."

When they were on their way home, she couldn't refrain from bringing up the subject that was on her mind.

"I wish you would tell me more about your experience

and the Bible that you seem to read so often."

His heart was thrilled as he realized that his witness for his Lord had not fallen upon barren soil.

"I'll be happy to tell you how I became interested in reading it, but I don't want to bore you," he said.

"I won't be bored. Please tell me," she urged.

"I began to read the Bible when I was a little fellow at my mother's knee. She helped me with the hard words and explained the meaning of what I was reading. She was such a gentle, patient, and wise person that I wanted to do anything that would please her, though I confess that I wasn't really interested in what I was reading. When I grew older and got out on my own, I'm afraid that I departed from what my mother had tried to teach me and I went my own way. But, as I later learned, she never stopped praying for me, though sometimes her heart ached when I showed such indifference to spiritual things.

"One day, however, I was made to realize that I was a lost soul and I asked the Lord to forgive my sins and save my soul."

He paused for a moment and she was afraid that he wouldn't go on.

"Please don't stop," she begged. "I'm so interested."

He gave her a smile. "I was just thinking of that scene beside my mother's bed. We all thought she was dying and all of us were there beside her, heartbroken and hoping for some miracle that would restore her to health. She called each one of us to her side and gave them a little word of blessing. All of them were Christians except me. She called me last of all.

" 'Dear Billy,' and her voice was so weak that at any moment we feared that she would stop breathing. 'You're my little black sheep. I love you, son, and I would give my very soul to know, before I go, that you're saved. I want to meet all of you when the Lord comes or when He calls you Home, but you're not ready to go. Don't break the circle. Give your heart to the Lord before it's too late.'

"I broke down and sobbed like a baby and I knelt there

and took my mother's hand and said, 'Mother, pray for me. I need your help.'

"She did pray and then she told me that I should pray and ask the Lord to save me and if that was what I wanted He would do what I asked. I asked Him with tears streaming down my face. When I raised my head again all the rest of them were crying but Mother, and she had a smile upon her face that I'll never forget."

"Did she die?" Loramie asked softly, forgetting what he had told her about his parents. There were tears in her eyes.

"No, she didn't. After I was saved, it seemed that a miracle really did happen. Mother dropped off into sleep with that smile still upon her face and when she wakened, she was stronger. The doctor was amazed to find her still living and from then on she began to improve. She's as well as ever today and still the same sweet Christian whom I adore.

"She gave me my Bible when she got well and I've read it every day since. As I said, the taste for cigarets was taken away soon after that, though I had a little struggle, for the nicotine had gotten into my system and the craving for it was there. I've never regretted the worldly things I gave up, for more wonderful things have filled my life since I surrendered it to the Lord."

"What things?" she asked in hushed tones.

She seemed to see that bedside scene and it stirred her strangely. How she wished that her mother was like this unknown mother in her dealings with her children.

"I began to attend Sunday school which I had forsaken long ago and I began to teach a class. I worked in a boys' mission until I began to study law. I wondered, when I was studying, if that was what the Lord would have me do and when I became ill and had to give up the practice I had started, I felt that this was a sign to me that it was not. I'm wondering now just what the Lord would have me do, for to please Him is the only thing I want to do. I gave up dancing, movies and cards which I had begun to enjoy. They seemed trivial and so unworthy of a Christian that I would have felt ashamed if I had continued spending my time with them."

"I think I'm going to have to get a Bible and begin to read it," she remarked.

"Would you let me give you one?" he asked eagerly.

"That would be nice of you," she said hesitatingly.

"I know you can well afford to buy one," he explained, "but it would give me such joy to give you one."

"I would love it," she said and gave him a smile.

He put out a hand and laid it upon hers for a moment as he murmured, "Thank you."

When he helped her out of the car at the foot of her steps, he said, "This evening has meant more to me than I can explain, perhaps more than you realize."

"I have enjoyed it more than I can tell you," she answered. "And I did appreciate your telling me about your being saved."

"May I come again soon?" he asked.

"Yes. I'll be glad to have you come whenever you have time."

"Then I promise it shall be soon."

She stood watching the car until it disappeared in the darkness. As she turned toward the door, she murmured, "What a man! What a man! I never knew anyone quite like him or quite so fine."

CHAPTER 7

A FEW EVENINGS later Loramie and her parents were sitting on the wide front porch with Darnell. They had just finished dinner and it seemed that none of them were in the mood for any lively conversation. Darnell was happy just to be near Loramie after a brief separation and Mrs. Herndon was quite pleased with his interest in Loramie which he made no attempt to conceal.

She felt that she had stopped what might have been a budding romance with Bill Fenner when she had dismissed him so rudely. She didn't regret her rudeness for it had been purposeful. She was determined that Bill would not be allowed to prevent any possible encouragement to Darnell.

While they continued talking and Loramie was at last getting into an interesting friendly argument with Darnell, much to the amusement of her parents, a car came up the driveway and stopped near the steps.

Loramie recognized Bill and she acted quickly to prevent an unpleasant scene, for she knew that her mother had not been aware that she had seen Bill again. She ran down the steps and spoke to him loud enough for the others to hear.

"Just wait a minute and I'll be ready to go with you."

He looked his surprise but said nothing.

"I'll explain later," she said in low tones.

"I want you to meet my parents," she said again in louder tones while she waited for him to get out of the car.

She led the way up the steps and introduced him to her parents. Mrs. Herndon acknowledged the introduction coolly, as if she had never seen him before. Mr. Herndon was cordial.

Darnell scarcely nodded and said nothing when he was introduced.

"Just a minute and I'll be with you," she told Bill and disappeared into the house where she picked up a scarf. She joined him again, before anyone had time to ask him to be seated, although no one showed any intention of doing this.

Bill felt very awkward and embarrassed, for he was sure that his presence was resented by at least two of the group, Darnell and Mrs. Herndon.

"Where are you going, Loramie?" her mother asked when she came out.

"Out for a ride, Mother," Loramie replied sweetly.

"But you have company," her mother informed her reprovingly. "You can't run off like this and leave Mr. Darnell. You can't be that rude."

"Sorry to contradict you, Mother," Loramie retorted pleasantly, "but Mr. Darnell is Dad's company, not mine, and I have no engagement with him, so I'm not being rude. Good-by. See you later," and she tripped down the steps, followed by Bill who felt very uncomfortable.

"Why did you do that?" he asked as they drove away, "and where do you wish to go?"

"One question at a time please," she said laughing. "I did what I did to try to make the best of a very unpleasant situation. I knew that you expected to call, but don't you see how very uncomfortable it would have been for both of us if I hadn't done what I did?"

"I certainly felt unpleasant," he said ruefully. "I felt that I was an unwanted intruder. I knew that your mother didn't want me to keep on coming, but I didn't realize that she disliked me so much."

"It isn't that, it's just that she has other plans for me," Loramie told him.

"I understand," he said with a chuckle. "That must be the man she told me you were about to become engaged to. Evidently her wish hasn't been fulfilled."

"No, and it never will," and her laugh joined his chuckle.

"That's a big relief," he said with an exaggerated sigh. "At least I won't be poaching upon another man's territory if I continue our friendship."

"Is that the way you regard me, sir?" she asked with pretended indignity. "Am I just a territory? I thought I was at least human."

He laughed again. They were both being silly, but they were enjoying it to the fullest.

"I suppose I just drifted into the jargon of my present position. Indeed you are human, one of the loveliest human beings I've ever known. What I meant and should have said was that I can at least hope, even if that hope is never realized. And now may I repeat my second question? Where shall we go?"

She knew that he had hastened to cover up his remark about his hope. She appreciated his tactfulness and contrasted it with some of Darnell's clumsy attempts to flatter her and to make her understand what his intentions were.

"Anywhere or nowhere in particular," she told him. "Let's just ride for a little while, or we can stop at some root beer place on the highway. It doesn't matter, just so we're together and away from that unfriendly army back there."

He gave her a quick glance and she was afraid that she had said more than she should have when he murmured "Thanks" as they drove on.

They came to a sandwich stand and parked nearby and waited for the waitress to take their order. She wanted nothing but a root beer and he ordered the same.

"This is a good place to stay for a while and talk, so I

won't have to keep my eye on the road," he said as they sipped their drinks.

"That suits me fine," she agreed.

"I brought you something that you said you wanted," he said later.

He took a box that lay on the seat between them and opened it, revealing a beautifully bound Bible inscribed with her name.

"I bought it in New Orleans," he told her, "and I had to have it imprinted with your name. It just came this afternoon and I was eager for you to have it."

She took the Book and opened it while her eyes glowed.

"How lovely!" she exclaimed. "Thank you, thank you! I shall always treasure it and I promise that I shall read it carefully and faithfully. You've made me want to know what's in this Book, for if it has made you the kind of person you are, I want to know something of its power."

"That's the nicest thing I've ever heard about myself," he said with a warm note in his voice and a light in his eyes. "I shall pray that it will do for you what it has done for me. May I make a suggestion? Begin reading in the gospel of John. I've marked it with one of the book markers. Then you can turn to the first of the New Testament books. If you wish, you may then turn back to the beginning and start with Genesis."

"I know that I may not understand what I read," she remarked, "for I'm as ignorant as you were when you were a little fellow at your mother's knee. It must be a Book of mystery and hard to understand."

"It's a Book of miracles," he corrected her. "There is enough simple truth in it to lead a seeking soul to salvation, but there is some deep truth that only a saved person can understand. That Word says that the natural man, that is, the unsaved person, cannot receive or understand the things of the Spirit, for they are foolishness to him, because they are spiritually discerned."

"I don't even understand that statement," she said.

"It means that until a person is saved, that is, until he

has confessed to God that he is a sinner and has asked the Lord to forgive and to save, he can't understand the deeper truths of the Bible. Many people say, 'I can't understand the Bible,' so they don't read it.

"Some are taught not to read the Bible," he continued, "and they are told that only one who has been educated in it has the knowledge to interpret it to his people. That's not true. Any one who has accepted Christ as his Saviour and is eager to know more about what the Word says, begins to understand it as the Holy Spirit makes it plain to him. The Bible shouldn't be interpreted. It should be accepted exactly as it is written, unless the plain context indicates otherwise."

"You make it interesting, yet you make it very difficult," she said in an uncertain voice.

"I shall pray for you that God will lead you to understand just what you need to know in order to know Him," he said with a tender note in his voice.

"I'd rather have you explain it to me," she said.

The tone of her voice and the look in her eyes told him something that caused his heart to leap joyfully. He began to have hope where there had been none.

"That would be a great pleasure to me," he said fervently. "But I'm afraid that it will be difficult, knowing how your parents feel about me."

"Only my mother," she corrected. "I'm not sure what Dad would think, for Mother usually has her way with him, but he isn't such a snob as Mother is. I hate to say that about her, but it's the truth. However, if you can't come to the house, I shall come to you. I'm not a child and I would be doing what would give me more in life than playing cards or dancing, or any of the other frivolous things that I've been doing all my life."

"I shall be happy to teach you what I know," he agreed.

They started back toward her home presently, riding slowly, then he turned off into a side road where there was less traffic and he could drive without having to look too closely at the road and the traffic.

"I believe you said your visitor was a Mr. Darnell. Am I right?" he asked.

"You mean Dad's visitor," she corrected with a smile. "Yes, that's his name. He's here on business for some fur company up north and he's staying at the house while he's looking over the territory."

"He's quite good looking and I imagine he can be very interesting," he said as he cast a sidelong glance at her.

"Yes, he is, but looks aren't everything. Personality and integrity count far more."

"The name sounds familiar," he remarked. "You said he was connected with some fur firm. He must be the one who has come here to look over this territory and obtain trapping rights to it. Am I right?"

His voice became serious and all the pleasantry had vanished from him.

"Yes," she answered, noting the change in his voice and his serious eyes.

"Then he's the one I've seen snooping around in my territory," he said. "I've kept an eye on him, for I was afraid that he was up to some kind of poaching, but I noticed that he had no gun nor any trapping equipment. I wondered what he was up to. Now I know. There was a rumor that came to me from someone who heard about him when he first came here. The trappers think he is here to try to invade their territory. Do you know anything about this?"

"I heard him say that his firm was interested in getting nutria fur and I'm sure that the people around here ought to be glad of that, for those animals are so destructive. At least that's what Mr. Darnell says."

"That's right, but there's so little in that trapping adventure here that the trappers aren't interesting in trying to trap them. There has been no market for their coarse fur."

"Mr. Darnell says that his company is interested in trapping them. They can use the fur and he is anxious to get as much as he can."

"That industry isn't enough to warrant his snooping around here," he argued. "He must have another motive."

"What other motive could he have?" she asked. "Dad seems convinced that he's telling the truth."

"Well, I'm not. I know this land better than your father knows it and that man must have some other reason for wanting to invade the trapping lands. Whatever his motive is, I'm afraid it means trouble for the trappers and if trouble comes, I shall do all in my power to help these trappers. They are so poor and they need this trapping to sustain them. Besides, they're my friends, and I shall protect their rights, no matter what it takes or what it costs me."

"I hope it won't mean trouble," she said. "That might mean that we can't be friends and I would hate that."

"You mean that if there was trouble, you wouldn't want me for a friend. That is, if I have to fight your father's friend."

"Oh no. I would still want you for my friend, no matter what would happen between you three, but I'm afraid that it would be very uncomfortable for me. I surely wouldn't want that. I'd hate to have to take sides against my father."

"I would hate that more than you would, for your friendship means more to me than you realize," he said seriously. "I'm sure that if your father should find out that this man wasn't what he pretends to be, he would be on my side and not on his."

"Let's hope there won't be any trouble," she said.

"Let's hope that there won't be," he repeated.

The lighthearted mood had vanished and they drove toward her home in a more subdued frame of mind.

As they parted, Loramie again thanked him for the Bible. As she mounted the steps and watched him drive away, she held the Bible against her heart.

CHAPTER 8

WHEN LORAMIE reached the porch, she was surprised to see both her father and her mother sitting there. She could see that her mother was angry and she observed the grave look upon her father's face. She said nothing, but waited for one of them to speak, for she knew that a storm was coming.

"I thought I made it clear to that fellow that he wasn't to come here any more," her mother said harshly.

"You did, Mother, very clear," Loramie told her, "and I'm afraid you were also pretty rude to him when you made it so clear."

"Then why has he persisted in coming here?" she demanded.

"Because I asked him to come. He told me that you had made it clear that he wouldn't be welcome, so I told him that whenever he could find time to come, we could go for a ride, so that he wouldn't be an unwelcome guest."

"Loramie," her father interposed, "I'm afraid you're making a serious mistake in disobeying your mother's wish that you shouldn't continue to see this young man. And I think he should take the hint and stay away from you."

"Dad, I'm not being stubborn," Loramie insisted, "but

I told Mother that I'm not a child and I think I should have the right to choose my friends as long as they don't bring disgrace upon any of us. I don't appreciate the way she treated Mr. Fenner. She treated him like he was some sort of a tramp, someone who wasn't good enough to be my friend. She even told him that I was about to be engaged to Mr. Darnell, when she knew that she had no cause to say that."

Mr. Herndon turned to his wife. "Did you say that?" he demanded.

"Yes, I did," his wife replied, somewhat flustered. "I thought that would give him enough sense to keep away."

"I'm sorry you told him that," and his voice reproved her. Then, turning to Loramie, he said, "I do think that you offended Darnell when you left him so unceremoniously. I'm sure that he was counting on an evening with you. I know that he admires you very much, my dear, for he made that quite clear to me."

"But, Dad, he's not my guest. He's just a business acquaintance of yours, whom you scarcely know. Why should I have to stay at home and entertain him?"

"Why should you insist upon continuing your friendship with this man who upsets your mother so much? She had higher hopes for you than to accept the attentions of someone about whom you know nothing."

"I know as much about him as you do about Mr. Darnell," she argued. "And that is only what he told you. I know that Bill Fenner is a fine man and that he has something that none of us have and that is a trust in God and an obedience to His will in a way I never dreamed of. He's inspired me to try to live a better life than I've ever known. He came here tonight to give me this Bible," and she held the Book up for them to see.

"This is the first time I've ever held a Bible in my hands. We've lived like heathen, with no knowledge of what's in this Book. He has made me want to find out what's in it and that's what I intend to do. He's promised to help me understand it better and I want to let him. I don't want to be disobedient, but I don't want to give up a friendship that means something so different from any that I've ever known. He didn't want to come here when he knew he wasn't welcome, but I insisted that he should come."

"This Bill Fenner must be a very remarkable person," her father said with a touch of sarcasm.

"He is," she stated, ignoring his sarcasm. "We are just friends and as far as I know, that is all that we'll ever be, but I'm sure that any girl would be happy to be the wife of a man like him."

"I think you should forbid her to see this fellow again," her mother insisted wrathfully. "I think this foolishness has gone far enough."

"Haven't you heard her say that she is no longer a child?" her husband asked with a sigh.

Sometimes his wife could be most aggravating and tonight was one of those times.

He knew why she was so prejudiced against this young man whom she scarcely knew. She was hoping that Loramie would fall in love with Darnell. He admitted to himself that he would be pleased if she did, for he felt that Darnell had wealth and position and that he could make her happy.

"You should let us move back to town. That would keep them away from each other," his wife insisted. "The servants could take care of this house while you're here and if she could get back with her friends, she would forget this presumptuous fellow."

Loramie smiled as she listened to this, even though it hurt her. They were discussing her as if she was not there or else as if she didn't have a word to say in her defense. Finally she intervened.

"You forget, Mother, that I still have my car, that is unless Dad should take it away from me in order to make me submit to your demands. Also, as long as I can drive it, I would be right back here. You can't punish me as you used to do, Mother, so just let's forget it and make the best of a bad situation. You are the one who is making it bad, and I assure you that I shall never do anything that would bring disgrace upon either of you, for I do love you very much."

She told them goodnight and went to her room, leaving one very unhappy person and another who was rather disturbed.

"What do you intend to do, Frank?" his wife asked when Loramie had gone.

"Nothing," he replied. "You can't use force with her or treat her as if she was a child. The more you try to keep her from seeing that young man, the more determined she will be to see him. Don't you realize that? Just let her alone and perhaps this situation will take care of itself. Give Darnell time and she may like him better than she does this other fellow. I don't think she would throw herself away on someone who wasn't worthy of her — a guard at the watchtower, for instance."

"I don't agree with you," his wife replied disconsolately, "but I suppose there's nothing that we really can do."

Loramie sat up late that night reading in her Bible. As Bill had suggested, she began reading in the gospel of John and as she read on, she became absorbed and interested and amazed at what she read. When she had heard the Bible read from the pulpit during the few times she attended church, she had either let her mind wander to other things or she had listened without really hearing what was read. Since the passages the pastor read were seldom referred to again in his discourse which was dignified by the term, sermon, she had no idea what the Book contained.

When she read in the third chapter, the passage containing the visit of Nicodemus, and what Jesus said about the new birth, she read that over and over again, trying to understand its simple yet deep teaching. She kept asking herself the same question that Nicodemus had asked. Just what did it mean to be born again? She was provoked at her own stupidity and she was eager for the opportunity to go to the tower and have Bill explain it to her.

The next morning Darnell was a pleasant as usual and Loramie was relieved to see that he didn't seem to be angry by her sudden departure the night before. She responded to his lively and sometimes gay conversation and they laughed at each other while her parents joined in the laughter and her mother bore a pleased expression upon her face.

"Would you give me the pleasure of taking you for a ride in the speed boat this afternoon?" he asked as they were leaving the table.

Loramie was sorry that he had asked, for she had hoped to visit Bill and have him help her with her Bible. But she thought that perhaps if she accepted Darnell's offer, there might be peace in the family. She could see Bill another time. She told him that she would go with him.

They left in the early afternoon. Though the day was warm, there was a hood over the boat and there was a breeze blowing, so they were not uncomfortable. They rode slowly along in the launch over the waters of the bayou. Blue hyacinths were blooming near the shore, while the gray moss hanging from the trees dipped slender tendrils into the waters.

As they neared the watchtower, Loramie strained her eyes to catch a glimpse of Bill. She wished that she could wave to him, for she knew that he would be watching them through his telescope or his binoculars.

As they drew nearer, Darnell turned to her and said, "I believe the watchman there is your friend. He's the one you went out with last night, isn't he?"

"You know he is," she told him.

"Have you known him long?" he persisted.

"No, just a short time."

"I suppose he's a friend of a mutual friend," he remarked. "Perhaps the one who introduced you two. I'm sure it has been lonely for you here, and I'm sure he's been lonely also. It was fortunate for him to have someone to introduce him."

She was provoked with him for his persistent questioning, for it was none of his business how long she had known him nor how she had met him. Evidently her parents had not enlightened him or discussed the matter after she had left with Bill. With a perverse spirit, she decided to tell him how she had met Bill.

"There was no mutual friend to introduce us, so I introduced myself."

"That was quite unconventional, wasn't it?" he asked after a surprised look.

"Yes, quite," she agreed icily. "I met him as he was getting into his canoe and I offered him a ride to town. He accepted my offer and so we became acquainted."

"In other places we would call that a pickup," he remarked. "I hadn't expected you to be quite that unconventional."

She didn't like his tone and it made her still more angry.

"But we're not in other places," she informed him in that same icy voice. "These people here are very unconventional and since I thought I could be of help to him, I offered to help him. I knew that he was trustworthy or he wouldn't be occupying such a position."

"He must be quite attractive to have aroused the interest of a total stranger."

She realized that it was jealousy that prompted him to say what he did and she smiled to herself. If he was jealous, then let him be. It didn't matter to her. It only amused her.

"He is quite attractive and one of the finest men I've ever known," she said. "However, I didn't discover that until we had time to get better acquainted. I am glad to count him among my friends."

She eyed him coolly and his manner suddenly changed.

"I missed you last night," he said in reproachful tones. "I was hoping that you would go for a ride with me, so we could also get better acquainted. I want to be your friend, Loramie," he said tenderly. "I'm sure that you are aware that I'd like to be more than a friend."

"This is so sudden, Mr. Darnell!" she exclaimed with mock coyness. "Do give me time to think it over."

He laughed and she smiled.

"But I'm serious," he said. "I'm sure that you know how beautiful you are and I know I'm not the first who has fallen a victim to your charms, so please don't joke with me. Do take me seriously."

"I am serious," she replied. "I've had no time to get better acquainted with you. You'll have to give me time for that. I like you, but just let's be friends for now, without a hint of anything more serious."

"Just as you say," he agreed, but he gave her a look that told her that while he was being obedient to her wish, he would still be intent upon more than friendship.

On their way back toward the watchtower, they met Bill in his canoe. Darnell stopped the launch and waited for him to draw near. Bill waved to them and gave them a smile as he stopped his paddling and drew along side.

"Mr. Fenner, I believe you met Mr. Darnell the other night, though perhaps you were not properly introduced. Or perhaps you were," she added as she remembered that she had introduced him. She was uncertain about that.

"Yes, I met Mr. Darnell," Bill said. "I'm sure that you're not poachers," he added with a smile. "but my duty is to see every strange craft in these waters and ascertain their mission into this sanctuary. I'm glad to see that you're on a peaceful mission."

"I assure you that we came in peace," Darnell said, trying to be pleasant, though Loramie could see that he was feeling far from pleasant. "Now that you know me and the boat, you can rest assured that it will always carry me on a peaceful mission and that I shall not be poaching."

"I hope that it will always be so," Bill told him, and his eyes were serious.

When they had parted, Darnell remarked, "He is quite a handsome young man. No wonder you picked him up." His tone was playful but it angered her.

"I don't like that remark, Mr. Darnell," she told him sharply. "When I picked him up, as you choose to term it, I wasn't thinking or caring whether he was handsome or not. If you want to continue being my friend, you will have to choose your words more carefully."

"Forgive me," he apologized humbly. "I'll have to admit that I was jealous when I saw how handsome he is. I didn't have time to really see him the other night. Believe me, I don't misjudge you. I think you're wonderful."

"Thank you," she said coldly.

The rest of the ride was rather quiet, for each seemed to be lost in his own thoughts and the desire for conversation seemed to have vanished. Loramie was glad when the ride was over and she had thanked him and had gone to her room.

CHAPTER 9

THE NEXT DAY Darnell left for another trip through the bayous that intersected the land surrounding the refuge. He didn't ask Loramie to go with him and she was glad that he didn't, for she would have refused to go. She didn't want to encourage him. Before she had become acquainted with Bill, she would have been willing to have at least a flirtation with him, making him believe that she was really interested in him. However, since she had known Bill even in this brief time, she had no desire to lead Darnell on.

She didn't try to analyze her feelings toward Bill, but she knew that he interested her more than any man she had ever known. Perhaps, she thought, it was because he was so different from any other man she had known. She knew that he had something that these others knew nothing about. Even though they lived in a land where the Bible was an open Book and where no one had an excuse not to become acquainted with its contents, those in her group of friends were as ignorant as she was and as unmindful of their soul's condition.

Loramie was impatient to see Bill again and to take him at his word to help her understand her Bible.

When her father and Darnell had left after breakfast, her mother became more agreeable and talkative than she had been since the night of their argument. She had been pouting ever since and had given Loramie the silent treatment. Loramie let her alone so that she could recover her good humor whenever it suited her. Her mother had often pouted whenever Loramie did something that she had not wanted her to do and Loramie thought it was better to have her mother pouting than quarreling and insistent upon having her own way.

She had not only experienced this attitude toward herself, but had seen it exercised upon her father who didn't always bear it patiently.

"I'm sure you had a nice time with Mr. Darnell in his new boat," she began as they left the house and sat in the shade of the porch. "It's a beautiful little boat and I know he's proud of it."

"We had quite a nice ride," Loramie replied.

"Mr. Darnell is quite an interesting person," her mother continued. "I never saw anyone who knew more jokes or could tell them in such an interesting way."

Loramie didn't reply for she was thinking, "Then I wish you'd let him entertain you instead of throwing him at me."

"I wish you'd be more friendly toward him, Loramie, dear," her mother continued in honeyed tones. "He's desperately in love with you. I can see it in his every glance. You never have had anyone who offered you more promise of happiness than he does."

"I'm not looking for anyone, Mother, with promise or without," Loramie answered rather impatiently. "Are you trying to get rid of me?"

"Of course not," her mother exclaimed. "However, when you do get married, I want your husband to be someone you'll not only be proud of, but who has everything that could make you happy."

"I promise that when I marry, the man will be someone of whom I can be proud."

She smiled. She was thinking that perhaps the man she

might marry would not be one of whom her mother might be proud. Not if she had Darnell as a model. Without realizing where her thoughts were leading, they turned to Bill and unconsciously her heart began to beat faster, a fact which surprised her.

"I'm sure that I can trust you about that," her mother answered in a relieved tone.

"I'm not in a hurry to get married, Mother, so please let's not talk any more about Mr. Darnell. He is, as you say, very entertaining and attractive, but I don't want to get married yet, even if he has any ideas as far as I'm concerned."

Presently her mother went inside and began preparations for a trip to the city and Loramie was left to herself, for which she was quite happy. When her mother suggested that she should go with her and visit one of her friends, she said she'd rather stay home and read.

Her mother gave her a surprised look.

"I never knew you were so interested in reading," she commented.

"I never had time before," Loramie told her, a fact which was partly true, for when she was at home, she was constantly on the go with her group.

She realized after her mother had left, that life was no longer as boring as it had been and that she no longer counted the days until they could return to their home in the city. She was counting how few days would be left of the present month and that after that there would be fewer still to remain here. Then she wouldn't be able to ride out and see Bill or have him come by to take her out for a ride. How time was flying!

She read for a little while, then after she had had lunch, she got in her car with her Bible on the seat beside her and rode out to the watchtower. She knew that Darnell was out somewhere in his boat and that he might spot her car, but she didn't care. She knew that if he did and if he mentioned it in the presence of her mother, there would be an explosion. She didn't want that, so she parked her car off the road in a spot that was partially hidden and not easily seen from anyone passing on the bayou. Then she got out her Bible and went to the tower.

Bill saw her coming and his heart stirred to faster beating. But there was something deeper than this fast beating of his heart everytime he saw her. There was the desire to be able to help her realize that she was a lost soul, beautiful as she was, and to help her find the way of salvation and to know the blessed peace that had come to him since he had received it from the Lord.

He waved to her as she drew nearer and went down the steps to meet her.

"Welcome to my humble abode, friend," he said gaily as he bowed before her. "I see that you have the password that admits you."

"Yes, the Word of God," she answered in the same light vein, then more seriously, "I've come for my first lesson, if you have time to teach me."

"Nothing could give me more joy," he told her and the look in his eyes sent a warm glow through her.

They mounted the steps together and she paused for a moment at the top, breathless from the steep climb.

"I surely must need more exercise," she gasped.

"These steps got me when I first began to use them," he told her, "but now I can spring up and down them and not feel out of breath. I'm thankful for that and for what this job has done for me physically, as well as the joy it has brought me in knowing you."

"My! You do say the nicest things," she said imitating a certain TV comedy character.

They both laughed, the happy, silly little laugh that bubbles from two who are happy just to be near one another and who are hiding their hearts' secret which neither is willing to admit exists.

He led her to the chair beside his desk and sat down by her. She laid the Bible beside his open one and turned expectantly to him.

"I've read this quite a lot," she said, "and I've found it

the most interesting book I've ever read. Yet there are so many things that I'm not quite sure I understand. I've just begun to realize how much I've missed all these years by not becoming familiar with what it contained. If I had not met you, I might never have known it and how terrible that would have been." She sighed unconsciously.

"Perhaps you don't know what I know so well," he said as his eyes looked into hers seriously. "That is, that all of this was in the plan of God for both of us. If I had not come here, I would never have known you and if I hadn't been so ill, I never would have come. And if you hadn't been here at just that time that afternoon, perhaps we never would have met. God is so wonderful to plan our lives as He does."

"Do you really believe that He does that?" she asked in surprise and with doubt in her voice.

"I know He does," he replied emphatically. "When you read further in the Old Testament, you will see so many of the things that God planned and how they worked out according to His plan. We won't take time to discuss them now, for I hope there will be time enough for that in the future, but just now, let me know what you want me to try to explain. I'll do the best I can and I shall pray as I have been praying. I have prayed that through our friendship and this Book, you may some day possess what I have, the salvation that God is willing to give to all who ask for it."

"I know that that is what makes you different from anyone I've ever known before," she said soberly. "I know that you have something that makes you different from what I am. For the first time in my life, I realize how shallow my life has been and how little worthwhile it is."

As she looked out of the window facing the bayou, she saw Darnell's boat drifting slowly along. He must have spotted the car parked nearby, for he let the boat idle for a while, while he took out his field glasses and examined the spot where she had left her car. Then he turned them toward the tower. Acting upon impulse, she ducked below the window, so that no one but Bill was visible. Then he started the engine again and rode away.

"Why did you do that?" Bill asked reproachfully.

"Because I didn't want to give him the satisfaction of seeing me here," she explained. "I'm sorry if you think I did wrong, but I know it's better this way. I'm not ashamed of being here, but it might make things less disagreeable at home. Mother likes him — well, I think you can understand."

"I think I do," he said. "She doesn't like me and she doesn't want her daughter to keep up a friendship with a lowly watchtower guard. Perhaps she's right," he added, "and you shouldn't come here if she doesn't want you to."

"I don't feel that way about it," she said emphatically. "I value your friendship and there is nothing wrong with being your friend. Your friendship is worth more to me than a dozen like him. No matter what position you hold, I realize as never before that character is what really counts and I know that you have that."

"I appreciate that," he said huskily. "Tell me what it is that you want me to help you with," he said, after a pause that was fraught with emotion.

She opened her Bible at the third chapter of John where she had placed a marker.

"I was interested in this account of the visit of Nicodemus," she said. "I was as ignorant as he was about the new birth. Though Jesus tried to explain it to him, I still can't understand it. He must have understood and been changed by it, for I read where he was there to help Joseph of Arimathaea prepare the body for burial. So perhaps I'm even more ignorant than he was, or else I'm just stupid."

He smiled. "You're not stupid. You just have never really learned what salvation means. You see, I was taught that simple yet wonderful truth when I was a child, so that it is no credit to me that I know it so well, even though it was so long before I accepted that truth.

"God's Word tells us that we are born a natural person, that is, we have physical life through our parents, but, according to God's Word, we are dead spiritually, for we have no spiritual life."

He turned to the book of Ephesians and turned to the first verse of the second chapter and read, "You hath he quickened, who were dead in trespasses and sins."

"That is proof that we have no spiritual life until God gives it to us. He only gives it to one who comes to Him, confessing that he is a sinner and wants forgiveness and salvation. When he does that, really meaning it, then God forgives him and gives him salvation and eternal life. This eternal life, which can only come from God, is the second birth. That person is then born again, or saved, or converted, whatever one may choose to call it."

"I always thought that being good was all that was necessary," she said, "and I never took time to think what being good really meant. I was taught that if we do all the good we can in helping our fellow man, and keep ourselves as good as we can, that we will be pleasing to God."

"No one can really be pleasing to God unless he has yielded his soul to God," he explained. "Salvation is such a wonderful thing and yet so simple. The moment a person really asks for forgiveness, he receives it. He has done nothing to merit it and he never can be worthy of it, but Christ paid for our sins when He shed His blood on Calvary. There is nothing for us to do but receive the gift which He paid for through His suffering and the shedding of His blood. He took our sins upon Himself and died in our place in order that we might not have eternal death, but have the free gift of eternal life."

She looked at him gravely and sighed.

"You make it so wonderful and yet so simple," she murmured. "It seems that all I have to do is to reach out and receive it."

"That's all you have to do," he said hopefully. "It's there waiting for you the moment you really want it and ask for it."

"I just don't know," she said sadly. "I don't know why there is no desire right now to receive it. Perhaps I'm not ready for it. Perhaps I still don't understand enough about it."

"I shall pray that the Holy Spirit will open your heart to the truth and give you the desire to accept it."

"Thank you. I hope that He will."

He took her hands and held them gently and looked into her eyes with a look she had never seen there before, a look which stirred her heart strangely.

"It would be the greatest joy that I could ever have, if I could lead you to the Lord," he said in low tones.

He bent and kissed her hands lightly, then released them.

She was touched and she felt strangely humiliated, as if she was unworthy of such an act.

They were silent for a little while, then he turned to another passage and began to read it to her. His voice was low and melodious and the depth of feeling that he put into the words seemed to make them stand out from the rest of the passage which she had read many times and it impressed them upon her heart.

There was a longing to be like him and to give him the joy he said he would experience if he could lead her to accept the Saviour whom he worshiped. But there was a coldness in her heart that baffled her and left her wondering, for there was no desire to do what she knew he longed to have her do.

Finally he closed the Book and she felt that she should be going.

"I'm afraid there will be trouble if Mr. Darnell lets Mother know that he saw my car," she said.

"I'm afraid there will be trouble from another source concerning him," he told her gravely. "I can't believe that he went to all that trouble and expense just to explore these trapping lands. He must have some other motive. But if he does try to rob these trappers of their rights, they will make trouble, serious trouble. I shall certainly do all in my power to protect them."

"I do hope there won't be any trouble," she said. "If there is any, believe me, I shall be on their side and on yours."

"Thank you. That gives me courage. I know I'll succeed."

He went with her to the foot of the steps and watched her walk away.

CHAPTER 10

THAT EVENING at dinner, Darnell was more amusing than ever. His little jokes and amusing experiences had them laughing frequently and Mrs. Herndon was delighted at Loramie's reaction to his humor.

Loramie noticed that even when he was laughing as he told some of his jokes, his eyes were fastened upon her speculatively and she fancied she saw in them a relentlessness that puzzled her.

Even while she joined in the conversation, she was thinking of Bill and what they had talked about and she was comparing these two men. What a difference! She knew that it wasn't only that they were so different temperamentally, but because Bill had so much more in life than this man had. Bill was full of fun, for she had witnessed his humor, but there was such a different purpose in his life. Darnell was bent upon only one thing and, as Bill feared, his purpose was to deprive poor people of a scant living in order to increase his own prospects of wealth.

She hoped with all her heart there wouldn't be trouble, for she knew that her father would be implicated with Darnell and she hated to think of taking sides against him.

After dinner, when they had sat for a while on the porch and the two older people had discreetly left Darnell and Loramie alone, they sat together in the swing.

"I saw your car hiding in the bushes when I passed the watchtower," he remarked as soon as they were alone. "You must have been visiting the watchman."

"What if I was?" she demanded, angry at his words and the tone of his voice. "Where I go and whom I visit seems to be my own personal affair."

"I suppose it's just the unconventional custom of this part of the country," he replied.

"I resent your words and their insinuations, Mr. Darnell," she said more angry than ever. "Our customs are quite as conventional as are those where you live. Even if my visit was unconventional, there was no harm in what I did and I shall do it again whenever I wish to."

He held up his hand and tried to interrupt, but she continued without letting him speak.

"It may help you to understand why I went to see Mr. Fenner. He gave me a Bible the other night and I asked him if he would help me to understand some passages that I couldn't quite understand. He offered to help me if he could, therefore I went to see him so that he could do that very thing. As you know, Mother doesn't want him to come here, so there's nothing left for me to do but go to him. That is my excuse for breaking the conventions so completely."

"I don't need any reason or excuse," he said. All the sarcasm had vanished and he was speaking humbly. "Forgive me, my dearest. I was so jealous that I couldn't help it. It made me so angry to know that you were there with him when I begrudge every moment that I'm away from you. I forgot myself. I've been seething with jealousy all evening, even when I was trying to be funny. Will you forgive me?"

"I suppose so," she said with a shrug.

"I want every minute of you, Loramie. I want all of you and I hate every minute that I'm away from you. I love you, Loramie. I love you as I've never loved anyone before. Please give me hope that you will try to care for me."

She was silent and after a moment of anxious waiting, he took her in his arms so suddenly that she had no time to resist, and kissed her roughly.

She released herself and pushing him away, gave him a resounding slap, then stood and faced him with anger blazing from her eyes.

"What gave you the idea that you had the right to do that?" she cried.

"I told you why. I love you. Have you never been kissed before?"

"Not like that," she retorted furiously. "That kind of a kiss is an insult."

"I meant no insult," he apologized. "I'm sorry if I offended you. I couldn't help kissing you. I love you so much, Loramie. Don't be angry with me, but give me hope."

"I'm too angry to give you anything, not even respect," she blazed. "I wish I could forget what you just did, but I'm afraid I can't. And don't you ever dare repeat the offense."

He faced her and there was determination in his voice.

"I don't give up easily, my dear, so remember that. Persistence sometimes wins over great odds and I shall be persistent, I promise you."

"I'm afraid you're due for a disappointment, Mr. Darnell," she replied coldly. "It takes more than persistence to win love."

With that she left him.

He sat down and remained there in the swing for a long time thinking. He was surprised at her reaction and he acknowledged to himself that he had misjudged her and that he had committed a grave blunder. He would have to change his tactics, but in the meantime he had more important things to consider. He had traveled through most of the bayou section that he was interested in and he had failed to find what he was looking for. It would soon be time for the trappers to begin to set their traps and that would interfere with what he was intent upon doing. They would have to be gotten rid of, for they might suspect that his interest was not in trapping nutrias.

In the meantime he would do all in his power to regain Loramie's friendship. He knew that this would take time and that as time passed he would be more and more involved in his undertaking. In the meantime he feared that there would be trouble with Fenner. He was not only jealous of Loramie's interest in him, but he was angry with Fenner, for he knew that Fenner would do all he could to oppose his efforts to rout the trappers from their territory. He had heard stories of others who had tried to invade their territory and who had met with injury or death.

He hoped to have the power to eliminate Fenner from the scene and to be able to take over without danger or harm to himself.

Not long after this he went with Herndon to New Orleans to begin his plea for exclusive trapping rights. It would have to go through the proper legal channels and he counted upon Herndon's influence to help him obtain his plea.

He had no opportunity to speak with Loramie, for she kept out of his way. At the table she was politely interested in the conversation, but was unusually grave, and her mother wondered what the matter was.

Finally, a few mornings later, he had a moment alone with her while her father was getting the car.

"Am I forgiven for my unspeakable rudeness?" he asked. "Please say that I am."

"Just forget the whole thing," she advised.

"I'll try, if you will too and if we can still be friends. I've been so miserable because you were angry with me. Please let us be friends as we were before this happened."

Just then the car came around the corner and he had to leave before she answered him. She hadn't intended to answer. She knew that she could never be his friend as she had tried to be in the past, for she no longer respected him. He was a ruthless person determined to gain what he wanted, no matter what tactics he used. How different he was from Bill who had kissed her hands and that so gently, when she felt that he wanted to kiss her as much as she wanted him to.

A little smile hovered upon her lips as she went into the

house. Her mother saw the smile and misunderstood the cause.

"I'm glad that you do like him," she said with a happy voice.

"I do," Loramie replied, still lost in thoughts of Bill.

"Oh, I'm glad to hear you say that," her mother exclaimed. "I was afraid that you didn't care for him at all. Mr. Darnell is a very fine man and I'm sure he could make you happy."

"Oh! Mr. Darnell!" Loramie exclaimed, then she caught herself abruptly.

"Who did you think I was talking about?" her mother asked sharply.

"I just wasn't thinking, Mother," Loramie confessed with a little laugh. "Of course Mr. Darnell is a fine man. He knows more jokes than anyone I ever knew. I suspect that he carries a little joke book and reads them so that he can spring them upon us."

"Oh, you ridiculous child!" her mother cried, laughing.

She led the way to the living room and Loramie followed her. She wondered what the future held. If there was trouble, how would it affect her relationship with Bill? She hoped that nothing would interfere with their friendship. She not only wanted him to teach her more about the Bible, she wanted to see more of him. Without quite realizing it, he had become the main interest in her life. She no longer remembered how she missed the old crowd at home and how she longed to return and once more be a part of it. All she wanted now was to see Bill, to hear him talk about the Lord and to see that look in his eyes that gave her a joy she had never had before.

CHAPTER 11

THOUGH DARNELL continued his trips through the marsh lands, he didn't invite Loramie to go with him. She was glad of this, for she didn't want to be alone with him and have to listen to his attempts to win some promise from her that she would refuse to make.

Before she had met Bill, she might have led him on before he had kissed her, just for the fun of it, but since she had known Bill and since she had been reading her Bible, she knew that she couldn't do this. Since that kiss, she didn't even want to be near him.

She remembered with a pang of regret and shame, the boys she had fooled when she had only been flirting with them and had no serious intention of falling in love with them. She remembered the disappointment and the reactions of others. One of them had become an alcoholic and had literally gone to the dogs in his despair and bitterness when his hopes had departed and he had realized just how she had led him on. She was glad that no one knew the real truth about what she had done. She wondered what Bill would think of her if he knew the truth.

Darnell frequently went to town with Herndon and

when they were at home, they were together alone in conference. Loramie thought that this must be in connection with his effort to obtain the trapping rights.

Mrs. Herndon was curious and asked questions, but her husband brushed her aside and gave her no answer to her questions.

Loramie was surprised one evening to see Bill's car enter the driveway. She wondered why he was coming when he knew that he wouldn't be welcome. He got out of his car and mounted the steps where they were all seated. He gave Loramie a smile, then turned to Darnell. She was wondering what she could do or say to meet this situation, but Bill spoke to Darnell before she could say anything.

"Mr. Darnell, I haven't been able to reach you by phone, so I thought it would be best for me to come here and talk to you in person. May I see you in private?"

"That won't be necessary," Darnell said coldly and loftily. "What you have to say can be said here. I don't think there is any need for secrecy."

"Very well, then," Bill replied.

He still stood there and, much to Loramie's anger, no one, not even her father, offered him a chair.

"Won't you sit down, Mr. Fenner?" she said and pushed a chair forward while she cast an angry glance at Darnell and a reproving one at her father.

"I'm sorry, Mr. Fenner," her father said as he rose. "Do sit down."

Bill thanked him and sat down opposite Darnell.

"I think you know why I've come," he began. "It's about the trapping rights you're trying to obtain."

"There's no need to discuss that," Darnell stated emphatically. "I have every assurance that my permit will be granted without any opposition."

"You're very much mistaken," Bill replied just as emphatically. "If you think you won't have any opposition to obtain an exclusive right to those trapping grounds, you had better change your mind. The trappers will fight for their rights, for it is their only means of support."

"That's just too bad," Darnell said sarcastically. "I'm sure they can transfer their energies to some other kind of work, fishing, for instance."

"That's ridiculous," Bill retorted heatedly. "Would it be easy for you to transfer your energies to some other kind of work?"

"That's beside the point," Darnell said angrily. "I represent a firm which will invest millions in this state from this fur industry. This small area is but a pinpoint in what we plan to undertake. It will not do your trappers any good to make a fight to keep my company out. This company already has the backing of Mr. Herndon and with his backing and that of his friends, I think I will get what I intend to have."

"If you insist in your demand to get exclusive rights to this area, I shall fight you, Mr. Darnell," Bill said seriously.

"You have no jurisdiction over any land but that of the bird sanctuary," Darnell informed him.

"But I'm a lawyer, and I shall give my services to these people to the extent of my ability, for they are my friends and I won't stand by and see them deprived of their rights."

"You, a lawyer!" and Darnell laughed derisively. "If so, why have you been forced to take the position you now hold? Evidently your profession wasn't good enough to attract a sufficient clientele to keep you going."

"Why I came here is my own affair," Bill told him. "I gave up my practice for reasons which are my own, but I do have sufficient knowledge of the law to know that you can't walk away with the grab you intend to make. I shall see that it is thrown into court, no matter what kind of backing you may have," and his gaze turned for a moment to Herndon who sat there with increasing surprise and uneasiness.

"Is that all you have to say?" Darnell asked.

There was less aggressiveness and also a lack of the assurance he had manifested in the beginning. Loramie noticed this sudden change.

"It is," Bill informed him in the same firm voice, and with that same grave look in his eyes.

He hated to be forced into this situation, for he realized

what it would mean. But he was determined to do all in his power to defend the men who were his friends and who were in danger of being met with an injustice for which there was no real excuse. He knew that Darnell could trap nutria without any need to drive the trappers out and that fact made him believe more strongly than ever that Darnell had some other motive in wanting the trappers driven out of the location of their traps.

He had a growing suspicion of what that other motive might be, but he gave no one a hint of his suspicions and he hoped that no one would suspect what he suspected. He wanted to wait and do what he had to do, if his suspicions were correct.

Bill rose to leave and said to Darnell, "I trust that you will reconsider your plan to drive the trappers out. You could obtain the right to trap without disturbing them in any way and there would be no trouble."

"I have no intention of changing my plans," Darnell informed him.

Loramie could see that Darnell was angry and when he was angry, his face was anything but attractive. How thankful she was that she hadn't fallen in love with him. She could imagine what a wife of his would have to deal with whenever he became angry. And, with a nature like his, so determined to get what he wanted and so merciless when it came to anyone standing in his way, there would be many times when he would be as angry as he was now.

As Bill turned to go, Loramie rose and went down the steps with him and walked to his car. Her father and Darnell watched her and Darnell's eyes lit with anger as he saw her stand beside the car and have a parting word with Bill.

"I'm afraid I've put up a barrier to our friendship tonight," Bill said sadly, "but I can't help but do what I feel I should."

"You have only made me more determined to be your friend," she told him. "I admire you for the stand you've taken, for I know what it will mean to take the fight to court. I hate to think that my father will be arrayed against you, but I shall be on your side, even though I can't give you any help."

"Knowing that you are on my side will be a great help," he assured her. "I need that moral support. I know that I have one other Friend who will uphold this just cause and defeat those who would rob these men of their living without any real excuse."

"I understand who you mean," she said, while her eyes shone. "I'll be out to the watchtower as soon as I can get away, for I want more instruction from a very dear teacher and friend."

He uttered a little gasp of surprise at her words.

"God bless you," he murmured. "Just remember that I shall continue to pray that you may have the greatest gift in the world."

"Keep on praying," she said as she then told him goodnight and left him. She was thinking that the greatest gift in the world for her would be to have his love, for in that moment she knew beyond a doubt what she had not been willing to admit before, that she loved him with a love that would be as abiding as it was strong.

There were stars in her eyes as she joined the group on the porch. Darnell saw those stars and they inflamed his anger still more.

Her mother looked at her and spoke severely.

"There was no reason for you to have gone to the car with that man."

"He's my friend and I think that's reason enough, Mother," she said with a lilt in her voice that even her mother's anger couldn't banish. "There was little enough courtesy shown him here. I thought he deserved something to show him that we do at least know what the word means."

"That man is due to cause trouble for us," her father said, "and if he takes this matter to court, he'll do everything in his power to make me look ridiculous."

He was concerned about his future political ambitions.

"All he will do is what he said he was going to try to do," Loramie asserted. "All he wants to do is protect the rights of those poor men who are his friends. Why should that make you look ridiculous?"

"Because I've already taken the matter up with the Governor and he sees no reason why Mr. Darnell's request shouldn't be granted."

"What does the Governor know about these men who are living in such poverty? Nothing at all. All he sees is the money the state might get for granting rights to the land that really belongs to them."

"You have nothing to do with this, Loramie," her father said severely. "I'm sorry we ever came here. I should have left your mother and you in town. I forbid you to have anything more to do with this fellow who's bent on stirring up trouble. Can't you see what it'll mean if he takes the case to court and defies me?"

"That word *forbid* is rather strong, Dad," Loramie told him. "I respect you and I love you and Mother, but I still feel that I have the right to choose my own friends. And Bill Fenner is my friend. I shall stick with him because he will need a friend. He has right on his side and I believe that God will take care of the right in this affair."

"That sounds like something you got from that fellow," her mother imposed. "You said he was teaching you about the Bible. Can't you see that he's just putting on an act to win your faith in him?"

Loramie couldn't help but smile.

"If he's putting on an act, I think it's a pretty good one. I know it isn't an act, for he lives what he believes. I never met a man who treated a girl with such respect, when he could have done otherwise."

She gave Darnell a withering glance, told them goodnight and left them.

Mrs. Herndon turned wrathfully to her husband.

"Are you going to put up with this rebellion of hers?" she demanded.

"What do you expect me to do?" he asked with a shrug. "She's the way you raised her — to have her own way. She's just showing the result of her early training."

"Well I never!" she exclaimed in hurt tones. "Blaming me for everything she does that we don't approve of."

"I don't think you need to worry, Mrs. Herndon," Darnell said soothingly. "She'll soon find out just what kind of a person this man is and she'll stand by her father when it comes to the pinch."

"I'm not so sure of that," she admitted dismally.

As they parted for the night and Darnell went to his room, there was a scowl upon his face, in spite of his soothing words. Loramie would be sure to find out what kind of person Fenner was. He would see to that. In the meantime he would exert every possible influence that money could buy to obtain what he sought — the riddance of the trappers so that he could be free to carry out his purpose in their trapping land.

CHAPTER 12

MORTON DARNELL had a sudden thought that gave him encouragement as he went to his room. He had been somewhat fearful that Herndon's influence would not be strong enough to outweigh an argument if the case was taken to court and Bill had assured him that it would be. But he remembered that Bill was not a native of the state and had possibly not established his right to practice law in the state.

The thought made his spirits rise. No matter what Bill tried to do, Darnell would see to it that he would not win any suit and that he would be out of Loramie's life permanently.

He had fallen in love with Loramie almost from their first meeting. This had surprised him, for he had been impervious to feminine charms, though he had had many affairs. As he knew Loramie better, her beauty not only made him admire her, but he had fallen in love with her almost before he realized it.

He was determined that this unknown man from nowhere should never have her, even if she did show so plainly that she was interested in him, if not in love with him.

The next day when they were on their way to town, Darnell mentioned the possibility that Fenner couldn't practice law in Louisiana. Herndon's face brightened at the suggestion.

"Why didn't I think of that last night?" Herndon exclaimed. "If I had, I might have settled the matter right then. I'll investigate, just to be sure that he's not qualified."

"I'm sure that he wouldn't have taken the trouble for that, if he was willing to take such a poor job as the one he has now," Darnell reasoned. "Evidently what law practice he had didn't pay off."

"Loramie said that he came from a prominent family and that he had entered practice as a partner of an established firm. He had to give up and take an outside job because of ill health. He got this position through a friend of his father's who lives here."

"That might not be the truth," Darnell remarked. "He might have made up the whole story just to make a good impression upon your daughter and to give as an excuse for his accepting such a position."

"You may be right, but I doubt it," Herndon replied. "Even though I don't like the idea of Loramie being such a friend of his, he doesn't strike me as someone who would make up a story just to impress her."

"She seems quite impressed, at any rate," Darnell said with a trace of bitterness which didn't escape Herndon.

"Yes, she does, and I don't like the idea at all, although there is nothing I can do to stop her. She's old enough to do as she pleases about choosing her friends, as you heard her say. She's a stubborn little rascal, but then she comes by it honestly. She's a lot like me and I can't help but love her for it, even though at times she does provoke me. But I know that I can trust her to always do the right thing."

"I hate to see her waste her friendship on that fellow who is bent upon trying to make us both look foolish if he succeeds in doing what he threatened to do," Darnell said disconsolately. "I don't mind telling you, Mr. Herndon, that I love Loramie and I could ask for nothing better in my life than to have her as my wife."

"That would please me," Herndon said with a faint

smile, "and I know it would make her mother happy, but as she said so forcibly last night, her husband as well as her friends must be of her own choosing. There is nothing I can do but hope for the best."

"But there is something that I can do," Darnell said to himself, "and I intend doing it if my chances don't improve very soon."

When Herndon met Darnell that afternoon he had bad news for him.

"I've investigated and I found that Fenner is a qualified legal practitioner in this state. He registered and took the examination when he first came here. He must have thought that he might need to be established here for some reason or other."

"That clinches it then," Darnell said dolefully. "He'll take it to court as he threatened to do."

"It wasn't a threat, it was a statement," Herndon corrected. "Somehow, in spite of my dislike of him because of Loramie, I can't help but admire him and his loyalty to his friends, men who can't defend themselves."

"He's persistent at any rate," Darnell replied.

He felt pretty much about Fenner as did Herndon. In spite of his dislike and his jealousy of him, he couldn't help but feel that the man had a sense of honor and a refinement that surprised as well as angered him.

That afternoon Loramie got out her car for a ride. Mrs. Herndon was preparing to go to town to some function of her club.

"Where are you going?" she asked as Loramie came out wearing her sun glasses.

"I think you know, Mother," Loramie replied, taking off her glasses and meeting her mother's eyes frankly.

"You're not going out to see that man after what happened, are you?" she demanded.

"Yes, that's where I'm going," Loramie told her.

"Have you no feeling for your father and what this might mean to him?" her mother asked wrathfully. "Have you lost all the love you had for him and have you no sense of propriety? What will people say when they know that you go there to visit that man?"

"I haven't lost any of my love for him nor for you, Mother," Loramie said. "As for the propriety of my visit, that tower is out in the open and in full view of anyone who cares to snoop. As long as I know that I'm doing nothing wrong, I can't help what people may say. These people are Bill's friends and they know him and trust him for what he is. I don't think they would put any other purpose in these visits, except what they are. Bill isn't trying to hurt anyone. He's trying to help those who can't help themselves."

"What if it ruins your father's political ambitions? Don't you care if that happens to him? He said that it might ruin his political future if the case comes to court. He's been trying to get this thing settled without any trouble."

"My friendship with Bill won't alter that. If Dad gets into trouble it will be his own fault," Loramie stated emphatically. "He knew in the beginning what it would mean to these trappers if he gets the privilege that Mr. Darnell wants. If that isn't right, then he has no one to blame but himself if he gets into trouble. I think Bill Fenner is doing a brave thing to fight them here where he has no friends but the trappers, and I want him to know that he still has me for a friend."

"You'll take sides with him against your own father!" her mother cried.

"Not in public, Mother, only in private. He will know that I am pulling for him, but no one else will know."

"Except your father, who will be hurt worst of all by your attitude."

"I'll be sorry if he's hurt," Loramie said regretfully, "but I can't change the way I feel."

"You're in love with him!" her mother exclaimed angrily.

"You're jumping at conclusions, Mother. We're just friends. Not a word of love has passed between us. He's the first man I ever knew who wasn't forward with me and trying to paw me about the second time I was with him. Bill Fenner is eager to teach me what he knows about the Bible which he gave me and which I've been reading faithfully. That's why I'm going there this afternoon, so that he can teach me more."

"I repeat that he's putting on an act just to win your admiration, though I can't see why you would admire that in him or anyone."

"That isn't true, Mother, and I think you know it. People can't put on a very successful act to fool people about God and their worship of Him. It can be detected by even the most ignorant. What he has is genuine and I would like to be like he is and to have what he has."

"You're impossible!" her mother exclaimed in disgust. "I can't see how you could have changed so in such a short time."

She flounced down the steps and Loramie followed soon after and drove toward the tower.

She was thinking of what her mother had said and uppermost in her thoughts was what her mother had said about her being in love with Bill. She had told the truth when she had said that there had been nothing between them but friendship, but she wished with all her heart that he would speak to her of what was in her heart and what she hoped might be in his.

She was sorry if she hurt her father, but she couldn't be loyal to him and leave Bill alone without anyone to stand behind him if there was to be a battle in court. He, of course, had the trappers as friends, but they were not quite the same kind of friend which she was. She felt that she was right in what she did and the statement that she had made to her father, for she felt in her heart that he was wrong in trying to help Darnell in his selfish and heartless scheme. She couldn't be on his side if he was wrong and if Bill was right and she felt that Bill was right.

Bill saw her coming and was at the foot of the stairs to meet her.

"I didn't dare hope that you would come again," he said with a happy lilt in his voice.

"Didn't I say that I was your friend and that I wouldn't

let you down?'' she asked with a smile. ''I told them all that much after you left.''

''I'm afraid it didn't make things happier for any of you,'' he said as the lilt in his voice vanished and he became serious.

''No, it didn't,'' she replied in the same serious tone. ''Dad thinks I've deserted him and of course Mother is angry with me.''

''And all of them dislike me and Darnell hates me,'' he told her.

''I don't think Dad dislikes you and Mother only dislikes you because she thinks I value your friendship more than I do Mr. Darnell's. As for him, it doesn't matter what he thinks about anything.''

''He's in love with you,'' Bill stated.

They reached the top of the stairs and stood looking out over the tall grass that grew in the open space. Beyond they could hear the birds singing, while the sun cast a golden glow over the top of the grasses.

''What makes you say that?'' she asked.

''How could he help it?'' he countered.

He turned and led the way to his desk and motioned to her to sit down in the big arm chair at its side while he sat beside her. He saw that she had her Bible and he smiled while a happy glow spread through his heart.

''Have you come for another lesson, Miss?'' he asked primly.

She laughed, ''Yes, I have, professor. I was reading over here in Second Corinthians and I wonder if you could make it a little clearer to me. I'm afraid I wouldn't make a passing grade in an examination upon that passage.''

He opened the Book at the passage she mentioned. He knew what it was, for it was familiar to him. It was a passage in the sixth chapter which contained the fourteenth verse. He read it aloud.

''Be ye not unequally yoked together with unbelievers, for what fellowship hath righteousness with unrighteousness and what communion hath light with darkness?''

"Does that mean that a person who is a believer can't even be friends with someone who isn't?" she asked. "That seems to me to make the believer think he is just a little better than the other one."

"But isn't he?" he asked with a faint smile. "He's better, not in himself, for he has nothing of himself to boast of, but because he is a believer. He has God as his Father and the other person has nothing, no matter how rich or how famous he might be. It doesn't mean that he can't be friends with that other person, but it does mean that he can't go along with the old crowd, for either he will be led astray by them, or else the old crowd will no longer want him."

"A person who obeys that command must lead a pretty lonely life," she commented, and he could see that the Christian life had suddenly lost its appeal to her.

"On the contrary, it is a fuller life than it ever was before. A person finds Christian friends who are much more satisfying than those others who are only living for the present and only want to have a good time. God has a wonderful way of providing better things for His children than what they had to give up because they chose to follow Him and obey His commands."

"That refers to marriage also, doesn't it?" she asked. "Does that mean that a Christian shouldn't marry someone who isn't a Christian?"

"Yes, it does," he admitted slowly and regretfully. "So many times a Christian has married an unbeliever, hoping that after they are married one can change the other and lead him to the Lord, but so often it doesn't work that way. It brings sorrow and heartache, first because the child of God has disobeyed His command and then because there is friction between them which often causes disaster."

"I see," she said quietly. "It takes courage to be a Christian."

"It does," he agreed. "But God has promised to give us the strength we need and He has provided every armor against the attacks of Satan, who does his best to lead us astray from God's will. In Ephesians we read that we battle against the powers of darkness in the heavenlies, but if we have God on our side, Satan is powerless against us."

"Have you ever had to fight a battle against this command?" she asked, looking at him anxiously.

"If you only knew how hard a battle I'm fighting now!" he burst out unguardedly.

They were by the open window in view of anyone who might be near, and as he said that and unconsciously leaned toward her, they heard the sound of a girl's weeping.

Loramie looked out and saw the tall grass waving as if someone was running through it. She turned her grave eyes, which had wandered for an instant, back to his eyes and she knew what he had meant by that remark. Her heart stirred for a moment with joy, then a feeling of resentment rose within her. He was fighting against being involved with her! If that was the way he felt, as if she wasn't good enough for him, then they had both best forget it.

"I must be going," she said abruptly.

"I'm sorry," he said. "You're angry with me. Why?"

He thought he knew the reason he had hurt her, but the damage had been done and there was nothing he could do about it.

"What does it matter? What does anything matter?" she replied flippantly, trying to cover up her hurt and indignation.

When they reached the foot of the stairs, she turned to him and said, "By the way, I've stopped smoking. It was a struggle, but I've won. Will that be a good mark on my record?"

Her tone was sarcastic and it hurt him.

"It's a big step in the right direction," he told her, pleading with his eyes.

She told him good-by and went to her car while he mounted the steps and watched her ride away.

He had heard that wild weeping and had seen the grasses waving as someone sped through them. He hoped that Loramie hadn't heard, or if she had, she hadn't paid too much attention to it.

As Loramie rode away she was thinking about that girl's weeping. She wondered if he had heard and if he had, if he knew who it was or why she had been weeping. She remembered her meeting with the girl who had threatened her that day in town. Who was she and what connection did she have with Bill? Could she be the one who had been crying so violently? She wondered if she would ever know.

CHAPTER 13

WHEN DARNELL and Herndon returned from town, Darnell wore a satisfied smirk upon his face and he was unusually talkative and jolly, both at the dinner table and afterward.

"You look like the cat that swallowed the canary," Loramie remarked as they sat outside. Her parents had gone inside and Loramie was forced to remain with him or else be quite rude by leaving him there alone.

He laughed. "That's quite a comparison," he replied. "I am especially pleased over the situation about those trapping rights. We had a conference today with the conservation board who were all present for the first time, and they gave me a favorable report. They were inclined to consider my offer for the exclusive rights to the section where I want my traps. I was rather doubtful, though hopeful, I'll confess, until today. Now I have every reason to believe that after they have another meeting, my request will be granted."

"But that will leave the trappers without any chance to make a living," she said, remembering Bill's words.

"Not entirely. The field is open to them elsewhere. This isn't the only section where they can trap for muskrats. It will simply mean a change of location."

"But it does mean that they'll have to move and how can they do that?" she argued. "They've lived here all of their lives, and they wouldn't be happy anywhere else. Besides, they don't have the money to move. They own their little homes, shabby as some of them are, and they couldn't build new ones or pay rent."

"That will be up to them, I'm sorry to say," Darnel said. "What my company will pay will mean more to the state than they now have. I happen to know that the state is in sore need of money, for they are already in the red and the year isn't half over."

"I think that's cruel and unjust," she burst out heatedly "I don't see how Dad could consent to such an arrangement I know he has more sympathy for these people than that."

"He's in a position where he can't take sides against me without getting in bad with the administration and I know he doesn't want that. Your father has ambitions, my dear," he remarked blandly. "He has no need of money, but he does have political aspirations."

"I don't believe that my father would compromise even for political power," she maintained. "If he takes a stand like that against these poor people, just for his political hopes, I'll lose some of the respect I have for him. I just can't believe he would do a thing like that. If he does, I'll still be on the side of the trappers."

"You've been listening to Fenner and believing he is right," he said reproachfully.

"I do believe he's right and I'll be on his side, even though it can't mean anything to anyone but myself," she stated.

"It will mean much to me, if I know that you won't be on my side," he said with purposeful wistfulness. "I'm afraid you haven't forgiven me for what I did. What more can I say to make you forgive me? I told you that I was sorry, very, very sorry. I wanted you so much that I forgot myself. It was no disrespect to you. I respect you more than any girl I've even known. I love you, Loramie, and I want you for my wife. Please give me a little hope."

"I'm not angry with you," she told him, "though I was very angry at the time. But I can't agree with you in what you're trying to do here."

"But you can be lined up against your father and he's with me. Can't you see how you will hurt him? And you will hurt me also."

"I'm sorry, but that's the way I feel and I can't change that."

"What can I do to make you feel more friendly toward me?" he asked.

"You can drop your plan to oust the trappers," she told him.

"You know I can't do that," he said regretfully. "I'm under orders from others and they're involved in this too. If it was only myself, I'd do what you ask. I'd do anything to win your love, but I'm powerless to do that."

"Then let's stop talking about it," she said in a tone of finality.

"You felt differently toward me until you met Fenner," he said bitterly. "Somehow he has hoodwinked you. He's put on some kind of an act to make you interested in him. He knows that your father is a wealthy man and he lost no time in winning your interest. He may be a fortune hunter, just trying to win you because he has an eye on your wealth."

"Thank you for the compliment," she said. "That's a contemptible remark," she added with a touch of scorn. "Bill Fenner isn't putting on an act and he isn't after my money. He doesn't need that and that isn't his only interest in life. He is what he believes and he believes in a God that I scarcely know. He's the finest man I've ever known and I'll stand by him in whatever fight he has to make to help these trappers."

"You really are in love with him," he remarked.

"I don't have to reply to that remark and I don't care to discuss it," she informed him coldly.

"Forgive me. I've blundered again," he said humbly, though he was feeling far from humble.

He was angry and jealous and he was more determined

than ever to do what he had in mind so that Fenner would be out of her life forever.

Just then her parents returned for a little time with them before they went to bed. Loramie was glad of the interruption.

The next evening, just at dusk, they heard the noise of shouting in the distance. They wondered what was causing all the excitement. They soon learned.

Down the road toward the house came a number of men carrying clubs and guns. They marched in orderly file, still shouting in their native French tongue as they came nearer. As they approached the driveway their shouting grew louder and more angry.

They marched up the driveway, brandishing their weapons. They stopped before the steps as they saw the three sitting there. Mrs. Herndon had stepped inside, but she came out and looked with frightened eyes upon the angry mob.

Their leader shouted in broken English, "We hev come for de one who ees tryin' to take away our beezeness."

Mr. Herndon rose and stood at the top of the steps as they milled about below. One of them raised a gun and pointed it at him, but the leader ordered him to lower it.

"What do you men mean by coming here like that?" Herndon demanded. "If you don't go away and stop that shouting, I'll phone the sheriff and have all of you arrested."

The leader laughed harshly.

"Whut kin he do eef he come?" he asked. "Eef he see so many, he'll run lak a rabbit. We come for de man who dey say ees tryin' to take away our traps from de bayou countree. Eef he don' leave and nevaire come back, we keel him!"

A loud shout greeted this warning.

"We don' leave widout heem onless he say he weel leave and navaire come back. He have no right to take away our livin'."

Darnell was visibly disturbed and Loramie could see that he was afraid, but he rose and stood beside Herndon.

"Dere he ees!" one of them shouted. "Let's take heem

out and geeve heem a beatin' and ef he don't leave, we keel heem!"

"Men! Please!" Darnell cried. "I'm not going to deprive you of your living and you won't have to stay out of your territory but a short time. We'll be able to work together as soon as we get our trap lines set."

"Dat ees one great beeg lie!" shouted the leader. "Ef we stay out ontil you get your traps set, what do we do for to live? You not come into our trap lines or we keel you!"

The crowd grew more threatening and Herndon wondered what he should do. He didn't want trouble and he had heard of killings in the past over such an incident as others tried to invade a trapping territory. He was afraid that something serious might happen to Darnell and if that happened he would feel that he was responsible for whatever happened to him while he was a guest in his home. He knew that the leader of the mob had told the truth. It would do no good to phone the sheriff. He could do nothing singlehanded to handle these infuriated men.

While he stood there a moment, debating what to do and growing more nervous as the men continued shouting and raising their weapons threateningly, he saw a car coming toward them at high speed. It turned into the driveway and stopped a few feet away. He uttered a sigh of relief, for he felt that help had come. When he saw who was getting out of the car, he had his doubts. How could he expect help from the man who had promised to fight in behalf of these same men? The man getting out of the car was Bill Fenner.

Bill rushed into the midst of the angry, shouting mob and shouted to them in their native tongue.

"Stop men! This is no way to settle this thing! It will only bring more trouble to all of you. I promised to fight for you in the right way, so trust me and go home and stop this unlawful attempt to take matters into your own hands. Let's wait and see what the commission decides and then we'll know what to do. Go home, all of you. Please!"

"But we heard from one of our men in town," the leader answered in French, "that that commission was going to give him what he asked for. That means that we'll be driven out and we'll starve before we can find any other work. That's the only kind of work we know and that land is ours to trap in. No one is going to take it from us."

"I promise you that it shall not be taken from you," Bill told him. "You have the land by rights that have never been revoked and no one can take it from you. I promise you that you will be able to keep your lines going. Now please go home before something happens that will drag you into trouble with the law. I'm your friend and I'll stand by you to the very end. Do go home. Renard, tell them to go home," he urged the leader.

"We'll trust you," Renard said reluctantly, "but if he wins, we'll kill him."

He turned to his men and told them to leave. The men reluctantly obeyed and followed him down the driveway and out to the road.

Bill turned to the two men still standing at the top of the steps.

"I'm sorry that this happened," he said to Herndon. "I came as soon as I heard that they were on their way here. I'm glad I got here in time."

"A fine lot of friends you have, sir," Darnell said wrathfully. "We might have been injured or killed."

"I don't think that would have happened," Bill told him, "even though they are a hot-headed people and they had a right to feel as they did. I shall do my best to fight for them," Bill told him, "but it shall be done through the proper legal channels and not with guns or threats. I don't blame them for being desperate, for you're trying to do a dastardly and heartless thing and I shall do all in my power to see that you don't succeed."

With that he turned and got in his car and drove away. He hadn't even glanced at Loramie and she felt hurt, even though she realized that this was no time for even a friendly glance, for he knew that he was in the presence of his enemies.

"How do you suppose those fellows found out what has

been going on?" Darnell asked as they sat down and he wiped his clammy forehead.

"I have no idea," Herndon replied.

"I've an idea that Fenner found out about it and that he just stirred them up so that he could come here and play the hero."

"That isn't true and you know it!" Loramie blazed wrathfully. "He's not that kind of a man."

"No matter what kind you may think he is, when a man's reputation is at stake, he'll do anything to save face before his friends," Darnell maintained.

"Is that the way you would act?" she asked icily.

Before he could reply, Herndon spoke.

"I agree with Loramie," he said. "I don't think he's that kind of a person. I think if he fights, he'll fight fairly, but I'm afraid that his case is lost before its begins."

"I hope you're right," Darnell said, as he rose and told them goodnight.

They all saw that he was shaken by what had happened. Loramie looked at him with contempt in her eyes. He was a coward as well as a heartless schemer and she felt that it would be difficult for her to even pretend a friendship she could no longer feel. He had lied to those men in the hope of saving himself from their intention to harm him. She knew that he had no intention of using the land for only a short time, but that his company intended to use it as long as it brought a profit.

He was a moral coward as well as a physical one. Perhaps before she had known Bill, she might have overlooked this, but now it assumed major proportions. He wasn't worthy to be compared with Bill.

CHAPTER 14

A SOLEMN-FACED Darnell met the family at the breakfast table. Herndon also wore a serious expression and there was little conversation during the meal. Soon afterward the two men left for town.

"We'd better get this matter settled as soon as possible," Loramie heard Darnell remark to her father as they went outside.

"We can't force the action of the board," Herndon told him. "They have the request under advisement and I suppose they'll give us the answer as soon as they have come to a decision."

That meant that there was a respite from immediate trouble and Loramie was glad of that. It would give Bill the time that he needed to make his plans in the event that Darnell's request was granted. She knew that he would do all in his power to prevent any further trouble or threats of violence.

She couldn't help but sympathize with the men, even though they had acted in the wrong way. Their living was at stake and she knew how poor they were and how desperate they must be at the thought of being deprived of their means of support.

She wanted to go out and have a talk with Bill, but she thought it wouldn't be wise just now.

That afternoon when both men returned from town and had nothing new to give them hope, she was glad. She tried to be pleasant to Darnell, since he was their guest, but she found it difficult and that evening she decided that she wouldn't give him the opportunity to be alone with her.

When her parents rose to leave them, she rose also and told Darnell goodnight.

"Please don't go," he begged. "Stay just a little while. I promise not to keep you long."

"I'm very tired," she said truthfully, but she joined him in the swing.

"I wanted to tell you how sorry I am about what happened last night," he began.

"So am I," she agreed, "but why should that worry you? You didn't have anything to do with it, did you?"

"Please don't be sarcastic. In a way, I suppose I did. But these men don't understand how much this means to my company. It will mean that we'll lose a lot of money if we fail to get what I've asked for."

"But the trappers will lose even more if you do get it," she argued. "They're not thinking of a lot of money, but of bread and butter, or even just bread. Don't you have any sympathy for them?"

"I do, and if we succeed in what we hope to do here, I'll see to it that they will have a share in the profits. I may even give them jobs when we get started."

"I hate to doubt you, Mr. Darnell, but I can't believe that nutria trapping will mean so much to your firm. If it had been profitable, don't you think these trappers would have been interested in it long ago?"

He knew that he had made a slip and he secretly cursed himself for this stupid blunder.

"The trappers haven't had an outlet for nutria fur. Our firm has just been experimenting with it. The belly of the animal has a soft beautiful fur and it has been made into a lovely coat so we decided to go ahead and trap on a large scale. This territory offered the best prospect. That's why we came here first."

He hoped that she believed him.

"And in the meantime? What will the trappers be doing while they're waiting for your bounty?"

"I'm sorry you don't believe me," he said in hurt tones.

"I'm sorry if I seem to doubt, but if this business will be so extensive, why can't the trappers do your trapping, instead of you bringing in foreign trappers and ousting these natives from their land?"

"I'm sure that this can be arranged in time," he conceded," but right now I'm interested in getting the rights to trap."

There was a silence for a time and she was on the point of leaving him when he detained her.

"I'm sorry I said what I did about your friend Fenner," he said. "It was inexcusable and I apologize."

"I agree with you that it was inexcusable," she told him. "Are you convinced that he had nothing to do with that mob coming here?"

"I don't know what to believe," he said with a sigh. "I can't imagine how they found out about the whole affair. If he didn't tell them, who could have told them?"

"They have friends in the city and at the capitol," she told him. "These people stick together and their representative from this district is a Frenchman. I imagine he keeps a pretty keen eye upon what might happen to affect the district he represents."

"I don't think that person could know about this particular matter," he argued.

"Mr. Fenner is not the only one who has seen you riding up and down through the marshes and they are not as stupid as you may think them."

"Let's talk about something else," he urged. "You have changed so toward me since you met Fenner and it hurts. In the beginning you showed a little interest in me, but since you've met him, you've grown so cold and indifferent. Why can't you be like you were before you met him?"

"Has it ever occurred to you that you might be the cause of whatever change you have found in me and that it is not because of some outsider?"

"What did I do?" he asked, puzzled. "You knew in the beginning why I came here and what I planned to do, yet you were quite friendly. In fact you gave me hope that you were interested in me."

"That was before I fully realized just what your plans might mean to these people," she replied. "I couldn't be in sympathy with what you propose to do."

"Who but Fenner could have given you that information and made you realize all of this?" he asked.

"Let's leave his name out of this," she said coldly. "I'm sorry, but I shall have to go. I'm tired and sleepy. I didn't sleep much last night. I'm tired of arguing, so let's just forget it. I can't fight in this battle, if there is one, but I can still be on the side of the right."

"I'm sorry you think I'm entirely in the wrong," he said as she rose to leave him.

"So am I," she replied. "But you have made me think that."

He sat there for a while, seething with anger and jealousy and the desire to do anything that would destroy this man who had not only proved to be a menace to his plans, but who seemed about to rob him of the woman he loved. Loramie's love meant even more to him than what he hoped to find in this strange marsh country, so different from the section where he had lived.

Loramie decided the next day that she would go to see Bill. She was sure that things had quieted down and that there would be no demonstration against her when she drove through town. She didn't think there would be, for she had made friends with some of the trappers' families since she had met Bill. They knew she was Bill's friend and she didn't think they would blame her for what her father was implicated in.

Not long before this had happened, two of the trappers had come to see Bill and had found them pouring over her

Bible. Bill had invited them to sit down and listen while he finished what he had been trying to explain to Loramie. He had been glad of the chance, not only to let these men hear something of the Bible, of which they knew nothing, but to let them see what he and Loramie did when she came to the tower.

She was glad that her mother was leaving this afternoon for one of her many social engagements.

"Please be a good girl and don't get into any trouble while I'm gone," her mother begged before she left.

"I'll do my best," she promised.

"And keep away from that man," her mother warned. "You see what trouble he already caused. Who knows what else he has up his sleeve to bring trouble to poor Mr. Darnell and your father."

"I'm sure that those two are well able to take care of themselves," Loramie told her.

Her mother looked at her gravely but she said nothing more as she kissed Loramie good-by and turned toward her car.

"I trust you, little one," she said as she got in.

"Do that," Loramie said and threw her a kiss. "I promise that I'll never do anything to bring shame upon you."

She felt a little guilty after all of this double talk as she got into her car and drove to the tower.

"I didn't think you'd ever come again, after what happened," Bill said as he met her at the foot of the steps.

"Why shouldn't I come?" she challenged. "I'm still your friend, am I not?"

"I hope so," he said with a sigh. "I'll need your friendship if trouble comes."

"Are you sure that trouble will come?" she asked anxiously.

"It's bound to come, for Darnell is determined to get what he wants and he'll use every means in his power to get it. I'm sorry that he has your father hoodwinked."

"Why do you say that?" she asked.

"Because I have reason to think that he's not what he pretends to be," Bill stated. "That's all I can say now and please regard this in confidence."

"I shall," she assured him. "I wouldn't repeat anything that might react against you. I want you to win because I know these men need you and trust you."

"How about me? Wouldn't you like to see me win, if only because I'm on the side of the right?" he asked with a smile.

"I want you to win for your sake first of all," she exclaimed impulsively and was immediately sorry that she had said it.

"Thanks, friend," he said, and laid his hand upon hers as they sat side by side at his desk.

She opened her Bible to a passage which had puzzled her.

"This mentions the return of the Lord," she said as she pointed to the passage. "It calls it the 'blessed hope.' Just what does that mean?"

"It speaks of something that's mentioned even more times in the Word than the Lord's first coming. It means that there is a day that God has appointed when His wrath will be poured out upon a sinful world where men have turned away from Him completely and are steeped in sin. Before that day comes, the Lord Jesus will suddenly appear in the clouds above this earth and all of the dead in Christ shall rise. Those believers who are still alive shall be caught up together with them to meet Him in the air to be with Him forever."

"When is that going to happen?" she asked. "I never heard that mentioned in sermons."

"This event could happen at any moment. Events are shaping up so fast in this old world, that it must soon go down the drain in utter destruction if the Lord didn't intervene. I'm sure that He will, before man completely destroys himself.

"From the word we have in prophecy and the way prophecy is being fulfilled, it can't be long before the rapture takes place."

"Then everyone who hasn't been saved will be left behind. What will happen to them?"

"They will be left to go through what the Bible calls the 'great tribulation.' Satan will have full sway over everyone and they will either obey his agent, the Man of Sin and take his mark, or they will starve or be beheaded. All this is found in the Book of Revelation."

"I started to read it but I couldn't understand it so I went back to the gospels. If that is true, it's a frightful thing."

"If it isn't true, then the Bible isn't true and if that isn't true, what do we have? Nothing."

"I was wrong to even mention a doubt," she said seriously. "I never knew what tremendous truths were in this Book until you opened it up to me. There is so much that I still don't know, but even though I can't understand, I can still believe, as you suggested. I believe it because you do and because of what it has done for you."

"That makes me very happy," he said in a voice that grew suddenly husky.

Just then they heard steps ascending the stairs and several trappers appeared at the door. Bill and Loramie smiled into the serious eyes of the visitors.

"Come in," Bill invited. "Miss Herndon and I were just having another session with the Bible. You've met her before, so sit down and feel welcome."

The men hesitated a moment and Loramie felt that they were wondering why she was there after what had happened. She rose and closed her Bible.

"I want you men to know that I am with you in everything that you're doing to try to save your trapping rights. I can't do much, but I am with you in spirit and if there ever is anything that I can do, I want to do what I can to help you."

"You can't do much with your pa on the other side," one of the men said. His voice was respectful, but Loramie saw a faint hostility in his eyes.

"I'm sorry that he's on the wrong side, but I believe he'll soon see that he is. He doesn't want to hurt you any more than I do. I'm Mr. Fenner's friend and I'll stand by you all the way through."

"Thanks. We believe you," he said.

She told them good-by and went toward the stairs.

She heard their voices raised angrily as she went to her car and she wondered if anything else had happened to stir them up. On her way home she thought over what Bill had told her about what he called the "Rapture." How wonderful to live with the assurance that no matter what happened to this old world, a person who was saved would know that he was safe in the Lord's hands. How terrible to still not be saved and to be left behind. And the Lord might come at any moment. Bill had that assurance and that was why he had no fear of the future, no matter what might happen.

That was why he wasn't afraid for these trappers. He had faith in God to know that He would answer prayer and protect them. Why couldn't she have that same faith? What was keeping her from yielding her heart and soul to the Lord so that she could possess that faith? She couldn't find the answer.

When she went to her room, she read her Bible for a long time. The more she read, the more unhappy and disturbed she became. Finally she closed the Book and went downstairs and began to play the piano. That didn't give her any peace, so she went outside and sat in the swing and tried not to think, but her mind kept returning to what she and Bill had discussed. She was sorry that the men had come, for there was so much more that she wanted to know.

Finally she went back to her room and lay down while she tried to sleep. She drifted off into a troubled slumber and was wakened by the sound of her mother's car.

For once it was a welcome sound. While she listened to her mother's account of what had happened in the city, there would be no time to think.

CHAPTER 15

WHEN THE MEN returned from town, they were serious and there was very little conversation both at the table and afterwards. Though Mrs. Herndon asked them what had happened, they refused to discuss the matter. Loramie felt as if she were a spy and that they didn't want to discuss the happenings in her presence, because they knew how she felt about the matter and how she felt about Bill.

She knew that her father was hurt by her attitude, for he had had very little to say to her since her outburst. There was nothing she could do about it but wait and hope that the trouble would not materialize. She couldn't even ask him to forgive her, since she still felt the same way and she knew he was aware of this.

She knew that her determination to be on Bill's side wasn't just because he was a friend of the trappers and was right in what he was trying to do. It was because she loved him and therefore she wouldn't desert him when he needed a friend to give him, as he had said, moral support.

She read again and again that passage in Second Corinthians which warned against having fellowship with unbelievers. She wondered if Bill really did love her, but that he wouldn't tell her so because she wasn't a believer. The thought hurt her and it also angered her, as it had done when he first explained it to her.

She longed to see him again, but she knew that she had no excuse and she didn't want him to think that she was pursuing him. It might be all right to go there when she really wanted to have him explain some passage, but she knew that if she went again now, it would be solely because she loved him and wanted to be near him.

She was restless and unhappy, and when her mother urged her to go with her to the city, she surprised her by agreeing to go. When they were on their way, she saw Bill's car coming behind them at a rapid rate. He passed them without seeming to see them. Loramie noticed, even in that instant when he was passing, the grim expression upon his face, and it disturbed her. She was sure that he must have seen her in his rear mirror and she felt unreasonably ignored and hurt. She knew that he must have been upon serious business and she was sure it had to do with the trapping situation.

"Wasn't that Mr. Fenner?" her mother asked as Bill passed.

"Yes," Loramie answered, keeping her eye on the road, for she was driving.

"He's determined to make trouble," her mother stated. "I hope he gets what he deserves."

"I'm sure he will," Loramie answered.

"He's determined to take this fight to court. Perhaps that's why he's on his way to town now. He's going to try to stop Mr. Darnell from getting those trapping rights."

"That may be up to the commission. Perhaps Bill can't stop them."

"I just hope he can't," her mother said.

Loramie didn't reply. She was hoping that he would succeed.

She was afraid of what might happen. Bill was determined to protect the trappers and Darnell was determined to get what he wanted no matter how he got it. She knew that her father had political friends on Darnell's side and she wondered what the trappers would do if Bill failed. They might do what they had threatened to do and this time Darnell would be at the mercy of the men and unable to defend himself.

She was so disturbed that she didn't enjoy her visit to the city, though she did have a chance to be with some of her friends. She was glad when they started back home.

Darnell and Herndon came in shortly afterward and they were laughing and talking and Darnell seemed to be in high spirits.

"You look as if something good has happened," Mrs. Herndon remarked as they came in.

"It has," he told her.

"That trouble maker has made his attempt to stop us and he's lost," Darnell told her. "I'm sure that from now on we won't have any more trouble from him. He tried to get an injunction to stop me from taking over the rights which the commission had granted me. He'll have to tell his trapper friends that they've lost. He made such a grandstand play that night and made promises that he knew he couldn't keep. He'll feel like a whipped dog and perhaps look like one to his friends."

Mr. Herndon finally interrupted him. Loramie could see that he was sorry that Darnell had said so much.

"Let's let the matter drop," he advised, then left them and went to his room.

Darnell turned to Loramie and started to say something, but she ignored him and mounted the steps after her father. He turned to Mrs. Herndon who was looking after Loramie with disapproving eyes. He held out his hands expressively.

"I'm afraid that I've lost something that means more to me than this land grant," he said regretfully. "She's turned her back on me."

"Don't give up," she advised. "Give her time and I'm sure that she'll change her mind and be more friendly. She's had some mistaken idea that she should stand by that man just because he has no one to stand with him but her."

"I won't give up hoping," he told her, and there was more than sorrow and disappointment in his voice. There was grim determination.

Loramie was so anxious to know what had really happened, that she decided to go to see Bill and learn the truth.

She found him sitting dejected and he was so preoccupied that he hadn't seen her coming.

"Am I intruding?" she asked as she stood in the doorway.

He looked up with a start and smiled at her.

"You never could do that." He sighed heavily. "Believe me, you're like a gift from heaven. I'm so glad you came. I need a boost just now and you're the very one who can give it."

"Please tell me what happened," she urged. "I couldn't get the truth from Mr. Darnell and Dad wouldn't talk. I wouldn't ask either of them. All I could gather was that you had tried to get an injunction and failed. Is that true?"

"Only partly true," he corrected. "I'm to get the decision tomorrow, but I'm sure that your father will use his influence to see that it is denied me. They will plead their case and make it look very good. I have no one to plead my case."

"What will you do?" she asked sympathetically. "The trappers expect you to win for them."

"That's what worries me. If they were not my friends, it would be bad enough, for I know how unjust this whole thing is, but they are my friends and I'm going to do everything in my power to help them. I haven't given up yet. I may have an ace in the hole, as they say, and I may yet give them a big surprise. I'll be in town tomorrow to get the decision and then I'll decide what I shall do. I'll be busy looking over certain records and then I may be gone for several days. I'll let you know just what happened and I do want to see you again before I leave. Much may depend upon what may come as a result of my absence. I have a man who will take over here while I'm gone."

"I'll come back when you return," she promised.

When she prepared to go, he took her hands and drew

her closer. She didn't resist him, but he didn't take her in his arms or try to kiss her. She was disappointed, for she longed for him to hold her close and to feel his lips upon hers.

"I've been fighting two battles, Loramie," he said in a husky voice, "one against this thief and one against myself. I wish that I could tell you about this other battle. If you can come tomorrow, perhaps I shall tell you. I wish that I had the privilege of seeing you in your home, but since this is denied me and you still want to come, I'll appreciate it if you do."

"I shall come," she said as she withdrew her hands and left him.

It was late when she reached the tower the next afternoon. The sun was going down and dusk was creeping among the trees along the bayou. She was expectant and excited in spite of her effort to tell herself how silly she was. She wondered if it was just a hope born within her or if it was something entirely different from what she hoped.

Bill met her at the foot of the stairs, for he had been looking for her.

"I can't stay long," she said, "for Mother and Dad will be worried about me. Mother is at home, but Dad and Mr. Darnell haven't arrived yet. I may be late for dinner, but that doesn't matter. I won't hide the truth from them that I have been with you."

"It may be for the last time," he said sadly as they stood just inside the door and opposite one of the many windows.

She uttered a little gasp and looked questioningly at him.

"I've lost the first round of my case," he stated. "As I expected, the injunction was refused. I'm sure your father and Darnell knew yesterday. If I don't succeed in what I have in mind, I shall resign my position here and return home, but I'm going to fight this thing to the limit. His face became more grave as he continued. "If I succeed in what I plan to do, then Darnell will be eliminated from the picture. If I fail, then I will be."

He came closer and took her hands again.

"There is something I must tell you before I leave," he

said slowly and with apparent effort. "I've wanted to tell you before, but I knew I shouldn't. I want you to know now, so that whatever happens, you will remember and not misjudge me. I want you to know that I love you, Loramie, darling. I knew for several reasons that I shouldn't tell you. There's no use going into those reasons now. Perhaps you know one of them. But I want you to know that I love you with all my heart. I've loved you almost from the first, but I knew that I shouldn't tell you."

"Because I'm not a believer," she said with a sad little note in her voice.

"That's the main reason," he admitted. "I've had such a battle with myself because I wanted to tell you how much I loved you and to ask you if you would ever be foolish enough to consent to marry me," and he smiled down at her.

"I understand," she said as she pulled away from his gentle clasp. "I know what the Bible says. You made that very plain. I'm not good enough for you because you're a real Christian and I'm not."

"That's not the way I feel about it. Not at all. It's just that I want to obey my Lord. That's why I've struggled against the longing to tell you and why I prayed so constantly that you would give your life to the Lord, but I can't go away and not tell you, for I may not have that privilege if I come back."

"I hope that you will come back," she said a little shakily. "Why do you say you may not come back?"

"I'd rather not tell you now. Just wait for me a little while."

He drew her to him and she let him take her in his arms. He pressed his sunburned cheek against her fair one and she let him keep it there, then he whispered, "Kiss me, Loramie."

She raised her lips to his and they met in a clinging kiss while her heart thrilled rapturously.

"Do you care just a little?" he asked after that wonderful moment.

"I care a great deal," she whispered.

Once more she heard the sound of wild sobbing and they were suddenly brought back to the present.

She withdrew from his arms and turned toward the stairs.

"I must go," she said hurriedly, for that weird cry had killed this moment of rapture while a vague fear entered her heart. "Let me know when and if you return."

He didn't descend the stairs with her as he usually did, but looked nervously out of the window when she had left.

As she went toward her car, there was a movement in the grass nearby and a girl's form suddenly appeared. She recognized the girl she had seen in the store that day. This time the girl carried a long knife. Loramie stood there transfixed with terror, waiting for her to move. She herself couldn't move a muscle.

"I tell you to leave my Billee alone!" the girl cried in a hoarse voice while her eyes blazed in the dim light and her face was contorted with fury. It was still wet with her tears. "I tell you I keel you ef you don' leave him alone. I see you kees heem. I keel you for dat! Billee belong to me. He's all mine. I belong to heem. I'm all hees and hee's all mine. I belong to heem, I say! And I keel you for try to take heem away from me."

Her voice rose hysterically as she advanced and raised the knife.

Bill saw what was happening and he raced down the steps and came toward them crying out, "Yvonne! Yvonne! Don't do that! Come to me!"

He advanced nearer and held out his arms.

"Come to me. Don't kill her. She doesn't want to take me away from you. She's just a friend. Come to me."

The girl hesitated and lowered the knife and Loramie fled to a safe distance, then stood in the tall grass to see what would happen.

"Eef she is just a friend, den why you kees her?" the girl argued as she went to him.

"Just a friendly kiss. Don't be angry with her. She won't take me away from you. Believe me, she won't."

"Do you lof me, Billee?" she asked.

"Of course, little one, of course I do."

"You know I lof you, Billee."

"Yes, Yvonne, yes," Bill said soothingly. "But if you hurt her, I shall be very angry. She's a nice young lady and you mustn't hurt her."

"I do what you say, Billee, because I lof you and you belong to me."

Loramie didn't stop to hear more. She sped to her car and started the motor and rode wildly down the road toward home.

Bill heard the car start and his sad eyes looked at it speeding away.

CHAPTER 16

As Loramie drove recklessly toward home, her mind was in a tortured turmoil and she was almost in a state of shock. She was remembering that scene of Bill with the girl in his arms, and the words she had spoken to him.

Anger and humiliation mingled with hurt pride and a hurt that was deeper than pride, the hurt to her heart when she realized what those words and that scene meant. The man she had admired above all others and to whom she had looked as someone as near perfect as weak humanity could be, had proved to be just another hypocrite and philanderer.

What hurt most of all was that he had won her love, a love so deep and so wonderful because it was given to someone of whom she felt herself to be unworthy. It had evidently meant nothing to him. If it did, he wasn't worthy of even her respect.

He must have been putting on an act, as her mother and Darnell had said, perhaps with an eye upon her father's wealth. The thought that brought shame as well as humiliation was the fact that she had, in a way, pursued him. At least she had made the opening for their friendship that had so rapidly ripened into love within her heart.

But Bill! How could he possibly have been so low and have been such a sham? She found it hard to believe that what he had taught her from the Bible had been only head knowledge, for it had seemed so genuine, as if he not only believed every word, but that he lived by the Book he had tried to teach her.

She remembered his tenderness and gentleness and his respect for her and the fact that he had never tried to take advantage of a situation that, to say the least, was quite unconventional. She had sought him out. He hadn't sought her, but she had justified herself when her mother had treated him so shamefully, in continuing a friendship which was so rapidly growing into love. He could have treated her as Darnell had done. She had fancied that she saw desire in his eyes, but he had been the considerate gentleman during all of their association. When he had taken her in his arms, she knew that he was aware that she wanted him to kiss her. His kiss had been tender, not the kind of kiss that Darnell had forced upon her. He just couldn't be different from the kind of person she had thought he was.

Yet she had heard and she had seen and she couldn't doubt the evidence of her sight and her hearing. That fact tore at her as she drove home and it brought havoc. She had stood by him because she had believed in him. He had just used her friendship in the hope that he might use her when he needed her, while he had been seeing this girl. He had lied to one of them. Which one was it? She asked herself that question a thousand times as she reached the town and sped through it recklessly.

It was even worse, she thought, if he didn't really love that girl. He had taken advantage of her love for him and if he had done that, he was lower than the lowest.

Life seemed suddenly to have lost its meaning. She could understand now why some girls killed themselves because the one they loved had proved unfaithful. In this moment of torture, she felt that she could lie down and die, for life would no longer hold any meaning for her. She couldn't face tomorrow and the tomorrow after that. She might have been able to face it stoically if Bill had died, but with this horrible truth in her mind, she felt that life would be worse than death. She hoped that she would never meet him again. Just now, in her bitterness she felt that she could use upon him that horrible knife that the girl carried.

She reached home just as the others were going in to dinner. She tried to slip upstairs without being seen, but her mother called to her and stopped her.

"Where on earth have you been?" she cried. "I was so worried about you. Hurry and join us or the dinner will get cold."

"I don't want any dinner. I'm not feeling well," Loramie said dully. "I went for a ride and I'm tired and have a headache."

"Let me send something up to you," her mother suggested.

"Thanks, Mother, but I don't want any dinner. I'm going to bed," Loramie said and continued up the stairs.

"I hope she's not going to be sick," Mrs. Herndon said as they went into the dining room. "She looked pale and not well at all. She wasn't feeling very well this morning. I could scarcely get a word out of her."

"Don't worry about her," her husband advised. "If she isn't feeling better by morning, I'll send for the doctor. Let's eat. I'm starved."

When Loramie reached her room, she shut the door and went to the table where her Bible was lying open as she had left it that morning. She had formed the habit of reading it the first thing after breakfast, as Bill had suggested, but while she was reading it the maid came to straighten up the room and she had left it lying there, intending to come back and finish reading it. Later she had begun to read it again and while she was reading, she came across the passage in Matthew where Jesus was rebuking the Pharisees. "Ye hypocrites! Well did Isaiah prophesy of you, saying, 'This people draweth nigh unto me with their mouth and honoreth me with their lips, but their heart is far from me.' "

Those words were so true. She read the passage over

again. So many people were just what those Pharisees were, hypocrites whose words and lives were so vastly different from each other.

While she had been reading, her mother had called her and she had left it open.

When she entered her room and saw it lying there, she went to the table and her eyes fell upon that passage which she had underlined, as Bill had suggested. He had said that it always called one's attention to it when she read it again and it would remain with her, perhaps when she needed it most.

As she read the lines again, a gasp escaped her. The words stared at her.

"That's what he is!" she cried. "A hypocrite. He had wonderful words but they didn't mean a thing!"

Suddenly she picked up the Bible and threw it across the room. It lay there with its pages spread apart like some wounded thing and as she stared at it, horror and shame overwhelmed her. That was the Word of God and she had done that to it! No matter what Bill had proved to be, he had given her a reverence for the Word and she had believed it and had treasured some of its promises and had memorized them.

She crept over to the Book and picked it up slowly and reverently and hugged it to her heart.

"God forgive me!" she murmured.

Tears filled her eyes as she laid the Book gently down and smoothed the rumpled pages, then she threw herself across the bed and burst into tears.

She didn't know what time it was when she undressed and fell into a fitful sleep. Her mother came into the room and saw that she was awake and asked her how she felt.

"I'm all right," she said, and she tried to smile, but the smile wouldn't come. "I didn't know it was morning."

"Your breakfast will be ready by the time you get dressed. Elsie is preparing it now," her mother told her. "I'm glad you're feeling all right. Last night you looked as if you were going to be ill."

She dressed slowly and went downstairs. She still

wasn't hungry, but she ate to please her mother. After she had finished, she went to her room and wondered what she could do to pass the time and to stop thinking. She wished she had gone with her mother when she left soon after Loramie had finished breakfast. It would have been easier to see her friends and pretend to be as gay as always, than it would be to sit at home and mope.

Presently she heard a car coming up the driveway. She went to the window to see who it was and she recognized Bill's car.

Bitterness, anger, and humiliation rose within her.

The maid answered the bell and came to tell her that a Mr. Fenner said he must see her for a few moments before he left town.

"Tell him that I don't want to see him, now or ever," she told the maid. "Tell him not to come here again, for he will not be welcome. Can you remember those exact words?"

"Yes'm," Elsie replied after a moment's wide-eyed stare.

Loramie listened at her door while the maid repeated her words and she heard the door close after a little while. She went to the window and saw Bill get into his car and drive away. She felt that all of her hope of happiness was going out of her life with him as he drove slowly away. It seemed as if he too was bearing the burden of a broken friendship and perhaps a shattered dream.

CHAPTER 17

AS SOON AS Mrs. Herndon returned from the city, she came to Loramie's room, for she was still worried about her. Loramie was sitting by the window, looking out upon the lovely garden with eyes that did not see its beauty. The sun was a red-gold orb in the western sky and the birds were singing their heartiest in the trees near her window. A mocking bird was darting down and threatening a yellow cat while it uttered harsh notes of warning, for there were baby birds in the tree nearby. At any other time she would have laughed at the antics of the bird and the cat, but now she seemed oblivious to both.

She was thinking of Bill and wondering how he had felt when she had refused to see him. She wondered how he could have had the audacity to come to see her when he knew that she had witnessed a part of the scene, at least, and had heard what the girl had said.

Of course he had come to try to explain, but what explanation could he make that he could expect her to believe?

She heard her mother return and she hoped that she wouldn't have to face her until she had gotten command of her emotions, but soon she heard her mother's steps in the hall and her knock upon her door.

"You look depressed and lonely, dear," her mother commented as she came in in answer to Loramie's invitation. "I wish you had gone with me to that luncheon. Some of the girls were there and you would have had a good time. Roger was there and he asked about you. He seemed disappointed that you weren't with me. I'm sure he would be coming here to see you if you would only give him a little encouragement."

"I don't want to be bored by him," Loramie replied. "He's about the dullest person I know."

"But his family is so prominent and he has a fortune in his own right. That ought to compensate for his dullness. I know that many of the girls find him attractive."

"Then let them have him. They're welcome to him. I don't want him."

"What is it you do want, Loramie?" her mother asked with a trace of irritation. "I don't understand you. You turn down eligible boys and give your friendship and interest to that fellow at the tower. I'm sure you wouldn't humiliate your father and me by choosing a man like him."

"You needn't worry about him," Loramie replied dismally. "I have no intention of humiliating you two on that score."

"Elsie told me that someone was here today and that you refused to see him. Could it have been that fellow?"

"Does that mean that you've had Elsie spying upon me?" Loramie asked. "I didn't think you'd do a thing like that, Mother."

"You should know that I wouldn't stoop to a thing like that," her mother said in hurt tones. "I asked Elsie if anyone had called while I was away. What I meant was the telephone. She said that no one had called but that some young man had come to see you and you had refused to see him. "I suppose it was Fenner. Am I right?"

"Yes, it was," Loramie admitted. "I didn't want to see him or anyone else. I was just down in the dumps."

She couldn't tell her mother the truth. She couldn't bear having her gloat over the fact that Bill had not been what he professed to be.

"He certainly had his nerve to come here after I made it plain to him that he wouldn't be welcome," her mother said.

"Let's not talk about him any more, please," Loramie begged.

"Of course, dear," her mother agreed, though she was curious to know why Loramie was so suddenly despondent.

Her mother left to change for dinner and Loramie told her that she would join her in a little while. When her mother had left, Loramie returned to the window. She knew that her mother wondered what had really made her refuse to see Bill. She knew that she could never tell her. As she continued to think again of Bill, the ache in her heart increased. She couldn't hate him though she wished that she could. The memory of those moments in his arms and his kiss upon her lips still brought a thrill even though she had seen those same lips given to another.

She wondered if she would ever be able to forget that love. Perhaps in time her pride would come to the rescue and she could forget how much she loved him, but she felt that there would always be that sense of loss which was so acute just now and that there would be a desolate place in her heart and within her life for a long time to come.

The boys she had once thought interesting and with whom she had played at the game of love, leading them on just for the fun of it, now seemed so insipid in comparison to the man she wanted to forget. There was still the image of what she had thought him to be and though she believed him to be a hypocrite, she still loved him.

No matter what he was, he had taught her to love and believe the Bible.

She rose slowly and wearily and went to the table where she had put her Bible and took it up reverently and opened its pages at random.

"I'm sorry I treated you so shamefully, blessed Book,"

she murmured. "I feel as if God will punish me for dishonoring His Word like that."

She didn't realize why she was looking through the Book. It was an almost unconscious urge that made her turn page after page. As she turned them, her eye fell upon a passage in one of the Psalms. It was the third verse of the one hundred forty-seventh Psalm. She read the words, "He healeth the broken in heart. He bindeth up their wounds."

She was amazed to find that verse and that she had discovered it at just this time. It was as if God had spoken to her from His Word. She read the verse over and over again as tears fell upon the page. She wiped them away carefully, then closed the Book and dropped to her knees beside the bed, sobbing great, tearing sobs that seemed to come from the very depths of her being, sobs that tortured her.

As she knelt there, she remembered how many times Bill had told her that he was praying for her, that she would one day know the peace that he had in his heart, when she would yield her heart and her life to the Lord. No matter what he might have proved to be, what he had done for her was something greater than anything she had ever experienced before. He had given her a knowledge of God that she had never had before. He had made her realize that God was a real personality, not just a name, and now this God whom she had longed to know in a more personal way was promising to heal her broken heart and to bind up her wound, a wound which she had believed incurable.

She had never prayed in her life that she could remember, and she didn't know how to start, though she had heard Bill pray once or twice before he had tried to open the Word to her. However she wanted desperately to talk to this God who was so loving and so merciful and she began with stammering words to talk to Him as a little child might talk to its mother.

"Lord, I don't know how to pray," she murmured through her tears, "but I want to talk to You and tell You how I feel. I know You know already, but I want to tell you that my heart is broken and I just can't go on if You don't heal this terrible wound in my heart like You said You would in Your Word. I believe that Word, Lord. Even though Bill isn't what I thought he was, he taught me to love Your Word and to believe it and I'm asking You right now, Lord, to heal my broken heart. I know I don't deserve anything from You, because I don't belong to You. I'm not a real Christian, but oh, Lord, I want to be! I want what I thought Bill had. I want to turn my soul and my life over to You. Forgive me for being such an indifferent sinner and save my soul, for Jesus' sake. I have to have You, Lord, because I can't go on without You and the comfort that I believe only You can give."

She knelt there for a while until the sobs gradually ceased. She felt, though she couldn't understand how it happened, that her prayer had been answered. She no longer felt torn by sorrow and she knew that the wound in her heart was not as terrible as it had been. She felt the assurance that she had been born again, just as Bill had explained to her.

When she rose from her knees and went to the bathroom to wash her face, the torture was no longer there and there was a strange new sense of calm within her.

She whispered, "Thank You, Lord," and freshened up a bit before she went downstairs.

For the moment, she had forgotten Bill. Her thoughts were filled with this marvel of the strange new warmth that had entered her heart, the unaccountable belief that all would be well with her, no matter what might come.

She was glad that the men had arrived by the time she went downstairs. She didn't talk much at the table, but her mother noted with relief that she no longer looked so unhappy. She heard her father and Darnell rejoicing that Bill's attempt to stop proceedings had failed, that his injunction had been refused. Now Darnell could go ahead with his plans. They would take precaution against any further attempts of violence among the trappers.

While Loramie listened, she hoped that their plans would fail and that God would protect the trappers. She had a conviction that surprised her, that somehow God would do just that. This gave her a thrill. She knew from what she had read and what Bill had told her, that this was faith. Now she had it! It was wonderful. She determined that she would never lose it, for she knew that it was the most wonderful thing that had ever happened to her, this new life and this new-found faith.

CHAPTER 18

THOUGH LORAMIE had found the Source of peace and though there was a new sense of security within her and the terrible bitterness had vanished, still there was hurt and doubt and disappointment. She tried to forget her love for Bill, but she found that forgetting was not so easy. She hadn't learned to pray for strength to accomplish something that was beyond her own strength.

She managed to appear cheerful, but within her there was still an ache and the battle against tears.

She agreed to go with her mother when she returned to the city. Anything was better than sitting alone and thinking. She met two of her friends and they went out to the lake for a swim, then they had lunch together at the club to which her father belonged. When she joined her mother for the return trip, she was in better spirits, for she had not had time to think. On the way home her mother kept up a continual chatter and Loramie forced herself to listen and not to think of herself.

"I'm sure you had a good time with the girls," her mother said when they were on their way.

"Yes I did," Loramie admitted. "It felt a little like old

times. I'll have to go with you more often, for it's lonesome at home."

"As soon as Mr. Darnell gets this affair settled and he can start work here, he'll have more time to be with you. Then you won't be so lonesome. Be kind to him, dear, for he loves you very much."

"I'm sorry if he does, Mother," Loramie told her, "because I don't love him and I know I never shall."

"I'm sorry to hear you say that, because I'm sure he could make you happy if you'd only give him a chance."

Loramie didn't answer and her mother changed the subject. She was glad when they reached home and the conversation came to an end.

Darnell was late. He had driven to town alone and he had returned just in time for dinner. His face wore a glum look and he had little to say at the table. Later when he and Mr. Herndon were sitting on the porch, Loramie heard them talking as she came downstairs.

"I don't like the look of things," Darnell was saying. "Fenner's a persistent meddler. He's been snooping in the survey records. When I saw him going into the record office, I followed him. One of the trappers was standing outside and when I came out there were two more there. They gave me a threatening scowl as I passed them. That fellow is up to something and I'm afraid there is going to be trouble."

Loramie didn't intend to eavesdrop, but she stood there without realizing that she was doing just that. Before her father could reply she joined them. She wondered just what Darnell had in mind if he was going to carry out his threat to stop Bill at all costs if he tried to interfere any further with his plans.

Her mother joined them and the conversation shifted to other subjects. When her parents rose to go inside, she rose too, but Darnell asked her to stay just a moment longer.

"I have tickets for a concert in the city and I wonder if you'd go to town with me tomorrow and have dinner and then go to the concert with me," he said.

"I'm sorry," she told him, "but I promised to go to see

the wife of one of the trappers. Her little girl is sick and I told her I'd come and visit with her for a while. The child is fond of me and I don't want to disappoint her."

She wondered if she was telling the whole truth. She had met the mother in the store and had promised to come to see the child as soon as she could. After what had happened, she had forgotten her promise. Tomorrow would be just the time to keep that promise and it would be a good excuse to keep from going to the city with Darnell. She felt a little guilty when she told him this, but she let it pass. It was partly true and she hadn't yet grown enough in her newfound experience with the Lord to be completely honest in everything she said.

Darnell showed his disappointment. "How about day after tomorrow?" he asked. "The tickets will be good for both concerts."

"I'll think about it," she told him.

She felt trapped and she wished she had consented to go with him the first time and get it over with. She had no excuse for refusing him outright, but she felt that she couldn't spend a whole evening with him and listen to what she knew he would be saying. Perhaps something would come up to keep her from going.

The next afternoon she went to town to see the child. When she had left, Darnell was still there. He got in his car and followed her, keeping well enough behind her so that she wouldn't know that he was following her. When he saw her enter the house on the edge of town, he parked his car nearby and waited.

It was dusk when she came out of the house, but instead of returning home, she drove toward the tower. When Darnell saw her drive in that direction, he went back into town and stopped at a small shop and went inside.

Loramie knew that Bill wasn't there and she knew that the sight of the tower would bring painful memories, but she wanted to go to her favorite parking place and sit there for a while, while she fought the battle that was still strong within her. She wanted to be alone where she could think, even though thinking brought pain. She still found it difficult to believe that Bill was what he had seemed to be. She wished that she had let him come in when he had tried to see her, just to hear what explanation he would try to make for what she had seen. But it was too late now. He was gone and he had hinted that he might not come back. He would have to be a closed chapter in her life, but she knew that it would be a long time before it was really closed.

Pain tore at her heart anew as she remembered the scene she had witnessed. Humiliation again engulfed her at the memory of herself in Bill's arms and his knowledge that she had wanted him to have her there and to know that her lips were eager for his kiss.

She heard a motor boat approaching and the sound roused her from her torturing reverie. She waved to him as she saw that it was one of the trappers and he waved to her. He passed her, then turned and beached the boat nearby, throwing a weight on the shore, attached to a rope from the boat.

As he came toward her she saw that he was a stranger and she wondered what he wanted.

"I saw you had a flat tire and I came to help you," he told her.

"Oh dear!" she cried. "I wonder how I got that."

"It's the rear right one," he said. "If you'll give me your key, I'll change it for you."

"That's mighty kind of you," she told him as she got out of the car and handed him the key to the trunk which she carried in her purse.

As she turned to close the door, in the instant when her back was turned, he grabbed her and almost choked her, while he held a cloth over her mouth and nose. She smelled the acrid scent of chloroform and she soon lost consciousness.

He put her in his boat and sped through the maze of streams that intersected that section. He finally stopped and lifted her out, carrying her unconscious form through the thick undergrowth to a small shack hidden in the tall growth.

He laid her on a crude bunk and had a few words with a

man who was waiting there for them, then he left, vanishing in the darkness.

When Loramie finally opened her eyes, she saw a man standing nearby, looking down at her. There was a dim light from a small candle nearby on a rickety table.

She stared about her for a moment dazed and wondering where she was. She tried to sit up, but fell back again, for the anaesthetic had left her still weak. She stared at the stranger and fear swept over her.

"Don't try to get up," he advised. "You won't be hurt. Just lie there and take it easy."

"Where am I?" she asked, looking about her at the rough boards and the roof that had holes in it.

"You're in a safe place until they come and get you to take you to where you'll never be found until we're ready to let you go," he told her. "He'll let you go when he gets what he wants."

"Who is *he?*" she asked as her fear mounted.

"You ought to know," and he laughed harshly. "Do you think Mr. Fenner would let that fellow take away the rights of these trappers? He'll hold you until that fellow comes to his senses and goes back to where he came from."

"What do you mean by that?" she asked, unwilling to believe what his words implied.

"Ain't it plain enough?" he asked. "I said these trappers are going to keep their rights to this land. Fenner said he would protect them and he's gonna do just that. When your pa knows what's happened to you, he'll make that fellow come to terms pronto. He'll see that this fellow gets out of here and gives up the idea of getting those trapping rights, or he'll learn that you'll never come home."

"Are you trying to tell me that Mr. Fenner has had this done to me?" she cried. "I can't believe he'd stoop that low."

"That's up to you," he said with a shrug. "He swore that he'd protect these trappers. He tried everything else, so this is the only thing left. It's either you or that fellow Darnell. It's up to your old man to decide."

"So that's why he went away," she said sadly to herself. "How could he do this to me?"

"Sure he went away," he said, for he had heard her. "They couldn't prove anything against him if he was away. Your old man will swear that he don't know who kidnapped you, that is, if he wants you alive."

"They'll get you, so you needn't think you'll escape punishment if any harm comes to me," she stated more boldly than she felt.

"You won't have that chance to see it," he said, "because if you're set free, I'll be long gone and they'll never find me. You just lie there and hope that nothing happens to you. I don't want to hurt you unless I have to. They'll be coming before long, to take you to where you won't be so easy to find if they start looking for you."

She didn't answer. She closed her eyes and lay there in a haze of torturing thoughts while the man went to his seat by the door and leaned back in the rickety chair.

CHAPTER 19

LORAMIE LAY there trying to understand what had happened and why Bill had done this terrible thing. He should have known that he would be punished and the punishment for kidnapping could be death.

Perhaps, she thought bitterly, he didn't care what happened to her, as long as he got what he intended to get for the trappers. Now that he knew that she was aware of the relationship with that girl, he no longer cared what danger she might be in.

She wondered just how he would be able to make a deal with her father, so that he would use his influence to get the privilege to Darnell withdrawn, or how he could persuade Darnell to give up and leave. She knew that this was done as a last resort to force the result that he could never hope to achieve otherwise. It was a diabolical scheme to use her and her father's love to coerce him into yielding.

She found it hard to believe that Bill would stoop to such a course.

She roused the guard from his dozing with a question.

"Doesn't Mr. Fenner know that he can't get away with a thing like this, that he'll be punished for kidnapping me?"

she asked. "Of course they'll know he did it, even if he wasn't here when it happened."

"He's a slick one and he's got it all figured out. Your old man will do as he says and give the trappers back their rights and he won't dare to try to have Fenner punished."

"How will he do that?" she asked.

"I don't know. All I know is what I had to do. When I get paid I'll skip out, and when Fenner gets what he wants, he'll leave too. Your pa won't have the heart to make any charge against him, he'll be so glad to get you back."

"It's a silly scheme," she told him, "and somebody's going to be hurt, because they can't escape."

"You just be good and lie there until they come for you, or it might be you who'll get hurt," he warned.

She closed her eyes again and tried to be quiet. She hoped that he would doze again, for if he did, she would try to escape.

After what seemed ages, she noticed that the fellow was beginning to nod. She raised stealthily, trying not to make any noise on the rickety bunk. She looked about the room in search of something that she could use as a weapon and she saw a big piece of wood on the other side of the room. The guard moved and she closed her eyes. He came over to her and she barely had time to lie down again before he approached. She tried to breathe slowly and regularly as if she were asleep, though her heart was pounding wildly.

He seemed satisfied that she was sleeping and went back to his chair before the open door. She opened her eyes cautiously and peeped at him. He had blown out the candle, but there was a faint light from the stars, so she could see his figure outlined in the dim light. She lay there waiting tensely for him to show some sign that he had dozed again. Meanwhile she wondered how Bill could have planned such a foolish scheme. Surely he had lost his head in his desperation.

Perhaps he did this to try to avoid bloodshed which he felt would be the result if Darnell persisted in his plan. She knew how hotheaded the trappers were, for she remembered stories of the past when there had been bloodshed over this very thing, when outsiders had set their traps in this territory. She wanted to give him the benefit of whatever excuse he might have for doing this. It was bound to fail and he was sure to be punished, for she knew her father.

Time passed slowly as she continued to watch the guard for some hopeful sign. At last, to her relief, she saw his head drop to one side. He drew it up with a jerk and then it gradually slumped over again.

This was her chance. She slipped off her pumps and crept over to where the chunk of wood lay. She waited a moment after she had picked it up, to be sure that the guard was still sleeping. Then she crept slowly to him, every nerve tense.

He raised his head with a jerk and she held her breath for fear that he would see even in that dim light that she was not on the bunk. His head slumped again to one side and she raised the chunk of wood, hesitated a moment, hating what she knew she had to do, then brought it down upon his head with a resounding whack.

The fellow slumped in the chair, then tumbled to the floor. She hoped she hadn't killed him, but she had no time to lose. So she took the revolver that he had dropped, put her pumps on and fled into the darkness. There was a faint light from a late rising moon, so she could barely see her way through the tall grass toward the stream, knowing that the guard's boat was still there.

As she crept along as fast as she dared, fearing that the guard might be restored and would follow her, her heart almost stopped beating, for she saw someone coming through the growth toward her.

She raised the gun which wobbled in her nervous fingers and put her finger on the trigger.

"Stop!" she called in low tones, "or I'll fire!"

Everything happened so suddenly that she never could give a clear account of just what had happened and how it happened. The man uttered a cry of surprise and held up his hands as he came toward her. In her nervous fright, without intending to do so, she pulled the trigger and the gun went off.

The man uttered a groan and fell to the ground. She ran to him, horrified as she realized that she had shot him, yet fearing that he might be pretending to be hurt, so that he could seize her. She knew that it was the one who had come to take her to a safer hiding place.

She knelt down, and as she saw his face, she uttered a low moan of horror. The man she had shot was Bill.

He opened his eyes for a moment, murmuring "Loramie," then he closed them again and lay still. She stared at him in horror and unbelief, then she began to cry hysterically.

She felt his shirt over his chest and felt blood. In that terrible moment when she thought she had killed him, she knew that, even now, no matter what he had done, she still loved him. But she knew that if he wasn't already dead, she must get him to a doctor. The problem was how to get him there. She ran back to the cabin and, to her relief, she saw that the guard had recovered from the blow. He was sitting in the chair, dazed and groaning.

"Get up and come with me," she ordered, holding the gun in front of her. "I've shot a man out there and I'll shoot you if you don't do exactly as I tell you. Come on out there and get that man into your boat."

"You hit me," he mumbled.

"Yes, I hit you," she told him, "and I'll do more if you don't do what I tell you to do. Get going," and she waved the gun in front of him.

He rose slowly and wobbled in front of her while she held the gun on him.

When they came to the still form of Bill, he looked down at him and cried out, "My God! It's Mr. Fenner!"

"Yes, it's Mr. Fenner, but you just hurry," she cried. "He got what he deserved, but I don't want him to die. Pick him up and take him to your boat. I'll get him to a doctor."

"I ain't going back there," the man declared. "They'll kill me if they find out what I did."

"You get that man into your boat and take us to my car, or you'll get what he got," she said fiercely.

She was desperately afraid and heartsick over what she had done to Bill, but she hid her fear from the man standing there.

"When you've put him in my car, then you can go and I hope I never see you again," she told him. "All I want is for this man to get to a doctor and for me to get back home. You can skip out as you said you would when this was all over. It's over as soon as you get him in my car. Get going!" she cried while she held the gun pointed at him.

He lifted Bill and half dragged him to his boat and they rode to where her car was still parked.

When he had put Bill on the back seat of the car, Loramie said, "Now get going. That beard may be a phoney or it might not, but I don't want to ever see you again."

She waited until he had gotten into the boat and rode out of sight, then she drove back to town recklessly and feverishly.

What followed seemed like a nightmare. She drove to the small hospital in town and Bill was taken to the emergency room while a doctor was summoned.

While the doctor was making a hasty examination, she went to the desk and phoned home. Her father and Darnell were out looking for her and her mother answered the phone. Loramie told her that she had no time to explain, but that Bill had been shot and she was with him at the hospital.

When she returned from phoning, the doctor told her that the injury was quite serious and that Bill would have to be operated on at once. He had only a fifty fifty chance for survival, for the bullet was very near his heart.

White-faced and trembling, she followed the stretcher into the hall outside the operating room. Then she sat down to await the result of the operation.

CHAPTER 20

LORAMIE HAD no idea how long she sat there waiting. So much had happened that she lost track of time, For a while, she waited calmly, for she was relaxed somewhat after the strain of her experience and was weary. She saw the nurses going back and forth through the hall and once a stretcher came out of one of the operating rooms. The patient's face was covered with a sheet and she knew that tragedy would meet the watchers who might be waiting just as she was. She grew sick with fear as she saw that stretcher pass her. She felt that she couldn't stand it if the one in room number three should come out with the sheet over his face.

Bill mustn't die! She couldn't stand it if he did. To know that she had killed him would be a scar on her heart that time would never erase. She would go through life accusing herself for killing the only man she had ever loved. Love like this would never come to her again. There might be other loves in a person's life, but there would always be the one true love that no other love would equal. She wouldn't ever want to love again. Even though he had proved to be unworthy of her love, it was still there in her heart which held such deep pain over his betrayal of trust and the humiliation of the knowledge that she had thrown away such wonderful love upon someone who had fallen so low.

Soon gray dawn began to steal into the corridor through the window at the end and trees outside began to take shape and emerge from dark shadows upon the landscape. She opened her eyes and realized that she had nodded from sheer exhaustion. She looked around, frightened and nervous. Suppose they had taken Bill out and she hadn't seen them? Suppose they had taken him down to the morgue to wait for whatever relatives he might have? They might not have known that she was his friend and the guilty one who had killed him.

As she sat there nervously wondering how she could find out whether or not they had taken him out of the room, she saw her father and Darnell coming toward her. They both looked pale and tired.

They hastened to her as she rose to meet them. She wobbled and caught hold of the arm of the bench.

Her father came and helped her to steady herself. He could see that she was almost ready to collapse.

"I got here as soon as I could," he told her, "after your mother gave me your message. We were out looking for you when you didn't come home. Someone left a note and rang the bell, then disappeared. Then I knew that you had been kidnapped. Darnell suggested that we should start out alone, for the note warned us not to notify the sheriff. We had to give up after a long search, for we knew that we could never find you in that maze of bayous.

"When we came back to get help, in spite of what the note had warned, your mother told me that you had phoned. What happened, honey? I've been almost out of my mind."

He led her back to the bench and sat beside her. She leaned against him and told him the whole story. Tears filled her eyes as she related her escape from the guard and how she had shot Bill.

"What did that fellow tell you?" he asked when she told him how he had said she would be taken somewhere else for safekeeping. "I mean did he give you any hint of why this was done and who did it?"

She hated to admit what the guard had told her about who was responsible, but she knew she would have to in the end.

"He told me that Bill Fenner had me kidnapped so that he could make a deal with you about those trapping rights," she said slowly, dreading every word.

"I can't understand why he should do a thing like that," her father said aghast. "Surely he knew what he was doing to himself by such a foolish scheme. He could be put to death for a thing like that."

"He may be dying for just that," Loramie said. Her voice broke and she kept back the tears with an effort. "I shot him and he may be dying, and I will be his murderer. That man said Bill could prove that he wasn't anywhere near here and had nothing to do with it."

"That was a crazy idea. I'm surprised that he would be stupid enough to think that he could make that stand before any court."

"If he was so far away, how is it that he was there when you were trying to escape?" Darnell asked skeptically. "He surely got back in a hurry."

"I don't know and I don't care!" she cried. "He's in that operating room where they've had him for ages. If he dies, I'll never forgive myself."

"Why should you care what happens to him, after what he tried to do to you?" Darnell asked.

"No matter what he tried to do, I do care," she cried. "If he dies, I'll be his murderer and I'll carry that horror with me for the rest of my life."

"It would be better if he did die," her father said. "If he lives, he'll be charged with kidnapping. I'll see to that. That was a stupid and cruel thing that he attempted, just to have his way."

"It wasn't that," Loramie argued. "It was to help those trappers to keep from being robbed of their rights. He wasn't thinking of anything but them."

"Evidently he wasn't thinking of what might happen to you," her father reminded her.

"Nothing matters but that he'll get well," Loramie said desperately. "If he gets well, he'll be off my hands and off my mind and perhaps I can have peace. Just now there is torture in my heart because I may have killed him."

"Come on, honey, let's go home," her father urged. "You need to get a good cup of coffee and some rest. Then you'll feel better. You've had a terribly trying time."

"I'm not leaving here until they bring him out of that operating room," she told him. "I've got to know what happens to him before I leave here."

"Then we'll wait with you," he said.

They sat there silently for a time, each occupied with his own thoughts and none of them were pleasant. Presently the door opened and Bill was wheeled out. Loramie uttered a prayer of thanksgiving when she saw Bill's pale face. At least it wasn't covered with a sheet.

The doctor came out soon afterward and spoke to Herndon, for he had risen to meet him.

"He's had a narrow escape," the doctor said. "He still isn't out of danger, but we got the bullet out without damaging the heart. Just a fraction of an inch nearer and he would have been killed instantly. Someone must have been a crack shot to have hit so close. He'll have to have nurses around the clock. Are you relatives?"

"No, just friends," Loramie interrupted. "He's able to pay for any expense, but I'll stand for everything. I brought him here. You see I shot him, but it was an accident."

The doctor gave her a doubtful look, then left them, after giving them the number of Bill's room. When they reached the room, Bill was already in bed with his nurse in attendance. The two men stood at the door while Loramie went in and stood beside the bed. Tears trickled down her cheek as she looked down at him. He had been so full of life and so tender the last time she had seen him and now he lay as still as death itself except for the shallow breathing. She turned to the nurse.

"How long will it be before he comes out of the anaesthetic?"

"I can't say," the nurse told her. "He was in severe shock when they took him into the operating room. It may be hours, or it may be less. He's still pretty low."

"I'll come back later," she told the nurse.

After one long last look at the still form on the bed, she left with the two men.

When she reached home, she was so utterly exhausted that it was all she could do to stagger up the stairs to her room. Her mother followed and told her that she would send Elsie up with her breakfast, but when the maid came in with the tray, Loramie was fast asleep.

CHAPTER 21

IT WAS ALMOST noon when Loramie wakened. For a moment she didn't know where she was. The night's horror was still with her and for a moment she thought she was still in that dreadful shack, not knowing what would happen to her. Then everything became clear to her and she remembered that Bill was there in the hospital, hovering between life and death, or perhaps already dead. She remembered that she hadn't once prayed during all this time of terror and mental torture.

She was still so young in her Christian experience that prayer hadn't become a habit, something to which she could turn in every hour of need. She rose and knelt beside the bed and began to pray with tears streaming down her face. She thanked God for delivering her from that awful terror, but she begged His forgiveness for shooting Bill. She realized that God knew that it was an accident, but she still felt heartsick and guilty about it. Then she prayed that if it was God's will, He would let Bill live, no matter what he was or what he had done to her. She asked the Lord to make Bill see how wrong he had been and that he would turn to Him and really be what God wanted him to be. She told the Lord that no matter how he had sinned, he had been the means of leading her to Him.

When she had finished praying, she bathed and changed her clothes, for she had fallen asleep without undressing. Then she went downstairs and admitted that she was hungry.

"As soon as I finish eating, I want to go back to the hospital to see how Bill is," she told her mother.

"Why do you have to go back there?" her mother asked. "That man doesn't deserve your sympathy. He deserves just what he got."

"I was the one who shot him, Mother. If he dies, I'll never forgive myself."

"But think of what he did to you and what he was going to do. He was going to keep you as a hostage to bargain with your father. I can't imagine any decent person treating you like that when you were such a loyal friend."

"I've learned a lot lately, Mother. I've learned that there is something more to life than just going along and living it in the way that brings the most pleasure. I've accepted Jesus Christ as my Saviour and I know what it means to have yielded my life to the Lord to use as He sees fit. I can't hate anyone, least of all, Bill."

"Don't tell me that you're still in love with him!" her mother cried aghast. "I knew you were, but I'm sure you can't love him now."

"That doesn't matter now." A sad little note crept into her voice. "All that matters is that I should live to please the Lord, for He has promised to be with me and to sustain me, no matter what comes to my life, sorrow or joy. I can spend the rest of my life trying to serve Him."

"Where did you get such ideas?" her mother asked, surprised. "I'm sure you didn't get it from that fellow. If you did, he wasn't giving you the truth."

"I'll tell you more about it when I have more time, but right now I want to get to the hospital," she replied.

When she had finished eating, she kissed her mother and murmured, "Don't be worried about me, Mom. I'll make you proud of me yet."

When she reached the hospital, she hurried to Bill's

room. The nurse was sitting beside the bed and she greeted Loramie with a smile.

"How is he?" Loramie asked, while she uttered a silent prayer of thanksgiving as she saw that Bill was still alive.

"He's still a mighty sick man," the nurse told her. "He's regained consciousness, but he's delirious in his wakeful moments. He's been sleeping most of the time. He keeps calling for someone by the name of Yvonne. Who is she?"

"She's a girl living near where he worked," Loramie told her. It was like a knife thrust piercing her at the mention of the girl's name. It brought back all the hurt and some of the bitterness which she thought she had conquered.

Presently Bill opened his eyes, but there was no light of recognition in them. He tossed his head from side to side, then cried out in weak broken tones, "Yvonne! Yvonne! What have you done to me? You've spoiled everything. I should hate you, but I can't. You're precious to me and I wouldn't hurt you for anything."

He rambled on, sometimes mumbling words that she couldn't understand and then crying Yvonne's name over and over again. Finally he quieted down and slept again.

When the doctor came in and got the nurse's report, he told Loramie that if Bill could hold his own for another twenty-four hours, he ought to make it. She tried to be glad, but there was so much hurt within her that she didn't much care what happened to her or to him. She felt cold and dead within.

Later on when Bill was sleeping quietly and the nurse told her that it was a good sign, she went home for a little rest, saying that she would be back later that evening.

At the door of the hospital, she met one of the trappers. She knew this man as one of Bill's best friends, Pierre Borsage. She had met him at the tower. He greeted her with a grave face and his voice expressed deep concern.

Loramie told him how Bill was and he asked if he might see him. She went with him back to Bill's room and he stayed a moment, looking down at Bill with tears in his eyes.

When they were on their way to the door, he asked if he might talk to her a while. She led the way to a bench and they sat down together.

"They told me what happened and that Bill was accused of kidnapping you," he began.

"How did you know that?" she asked, surprised that the news had gotten out so soon.

"We've been keeping track of that fellow who's trying to rob us," he explained. "Right after Bill was taken to the hospital, word got out among our men that this fellow was asking for Bill's arrest. News gets around fast here, since things are so stirred up. If Bill gets blamed for this, there'll be trouble, because we know that he couldn't do a thing like that."

"But the man who was standing guard over me said that Bill had paid him to do it," she argued. "I don't blame Bill without proof, but I have this man's word. He said that Bill planned to do this so that he could use me to make a deal with my father so that you trappers could keep your rights."

"That's a lie," he said. "Bill knew enough about that fellow to put him out of business for good and he wasn't worried about the outcome of this. It's a secret that only two of us know, and it'll soon come out when Bill's ready. But if Bill is accused of this crime while he's so sick and not able to defend himself, there's no telling what might happen. Can't you do something to save him?"

"What can I do?" she asked helplessly. "I'm willing to do anything to help save him from being punished for something he didn't do."

"We've got to think of something," he said. "We won't let him go to jail. There'll be some shooting if that happens."

"There mustn't be any shooting. Do warn the men not to start trouble. Give me time," she begged. "I'll try to think of something.

"If Bill gets well enough, we may get the truth," she

said after a moment's thinking, trying to fit the pieces of this puzzle together. "Keep in touch with me and if I can think of anything, I'll let you know."

He went away still worried, but promising to wait a while for whatever might develop.

When she returned later, the doctor found Bill much improved and he said that, barring unforeseen complications, he would recover, though it would take time. When she left the hospital she had a sudden idea, and she went to the home of Mr. Borsage. She asked him if he could take her for a trip on the bayou the next morning. They would try to find the shack where she had been kept.

She had no idea why she wanted to go to the shack, but she was hoping that she might find some clue that would give her a lead as to who had kidnapped her, if it really wasn't Bill. She still wasn't sure that he had not planned the whole thing. It seemed plausible that he had done it, from what the man had told her, much as she hated to admit it.

She smiled to herself as she thought of her plan to search the shack. That was what the detectives usually did in the TV crime stories. She wished that some of those detectives would come to her aid in real life.

When they were on their way in Borsage's motor boat, he asked her what she had in mind.

"I don't know," she admitted. "I'm just hoping that I might find something that would help us in finding the one who really did that thing. Are you sure that you can find the shack?"

"I can find it if anyone can," he assured her. "These trappers know every inch of this land. That's why they planned to take you somewhere else so that we couldn't find you."

As they passed the tower Loramie's heart throbbed painfully as she thought of the times she had spent there with Bill. Presently she saw the girl in the distance, standing on the bank of the stream. She was waving to them.

"Poor Yvonne!" Borsage remarked. "She's looking for Bill. I guess she's lost without him."

"She tried to kill me once and she may try again," Loramie said.

"She tried to kill you!" he exclaimed. "Why did she do that?"

"She said I was taking Bill from her. She said that she belonged to him and that I had no right to him."

"Poor Yvonne! She's touched in the head. She's always been that way. She's like a little child. Bill humors her because she's like she is. He feels sorry for her. Her father is dead and her mother has a hard time getting along. All of us try to help her."

Loramie listened as emotions rushed in upon her so that she could scarcely think. She had misjudged Bill because of this simple-minded girl who worshiped him. Why shouldn't she worship him and why shouldn't she hate anyone who threatened to take him away from her? And, after all, Bill was no hypocrite! He was what she had thought him to be, tender hearted and compassionate. And he loved her! So, he just couldn't have done that dastardly deed of kidnapping her. This was the truth that stood out like a shining emblem of hope in the midst of her whirling thoughts.

They stopped when they came to where Yvonne was standing.

"I'll bet you're looking for Bill," he said cheerfully.

"Oui," she said. "Where ees he? Who took heem away? Did you?" she asked angrily, turning hostile eyes upon Loramie.

"Non, cherie," Borsage said. "He went away on business, but he'll be back, so you just be a good girl until then."

She nodded and turned away, walking slowly through the undergrowth.

"Poor little thing!" Loramie exclaimed, her voice now full of pity. "I can imagine how she feels. She would feel worse if she knew how sick he is."

"I just hope that she doesn't find out that Bill is in the hospital, because she might try to find him and get lost. Before he came, she used to wander off and we had a hard time finding her."

All at once, all the hurt and doubt and bitterness had gone, and in Loramie's heart was a great peace. She knew that somehow God would set everything right about Bill, for she felt that he was innocent of the crime he was supposed to have committed.

The birds suddenly seemed to sing more beautifully and the sun seemed to shine more brilliantly and her whole world had taken on a new aspect. Life seemed wonderful again, even though Bill was still in a critical condition.

CHAPTER 22

AS THEY RODE away and Loramie saw Yvonne turn and give them a last look, she felt sorry for her. She had almost hated her before. Bill was all that this girl had and he would soon be taken away from her. That is, if they found him guilty of kidnapping. She hoped and prayed as Borsage rode slowly down the bayou.

"What do you hope to find in that shack?" he asked.

"I don't know," Loramie admitted. "I may not find anything, but that was the only thing I could think of doing, going back to the place where I was held prisoner. Something might have been left there that would help us identify the man who was my guard. Even though I hate to believe that Bill is guilty, still I can't see what motive anyone else could have for doing such a foolish thing. He ought to know that he would be unable to make the kind of deal he hoped to make, without incriminating himself and everyone connected with what he tried to do."

It didn't take Borsage long to find the shack. It looked even more dilapidated in daylight than it had in the darkness. It was well hidden from the stream and it was an ideal temporary hiding place. A narrow trail that was almost invisible led to it.

When they had reached the shack, Loramie shuddered as she saw the bunk on which she had lain, for it was unspeakably filthy.

They searched every inch of the place, which didn't take long, for the shack was quite small, but they found nothing that might help them.

"We may as well go," Loramie said in disappointment. "There's nothing here that would help us. I didn't have much hope, but it was worth trying at least."

Borsage led the way outside and after one last look around, Loramie turned to follow him. As she approached the door, she saw a bright little speck in a crack between two boards, that reflected the rays of the sun shining in the doorway. She stopped to see what it was, for it looked like a small jewel shining brightly. She picked it out of the crack and examined it closely, while her eyes grew wide and a gasp escaped her. The object she found was a little broken link. It was beautifully chased on the top. It was broken underneath.

At first she decided not to say anything to Borsage about what she had found, but on second thought she thought it was better to tell him. If the necessity should arise, he could be a witness as to where she had found it. Her face was grave as they got in the boat and Borsage started the motor.

"You look disappointed," he remarked as the boat got under way. "I'm disappointed too. What'll we do now?"

"I did find something," Loramie told him.

She took out the small link and showed it to him.

"I found it in a crack by the door, just as I was coming out. I can't decide what to do about it and it may not amount to anything, but I want you to see it and to witness, if necessary, that I found it here. Don't say anything about it until I know what to do and if I know that this is anything important. When I need you, I'll let you know. We may have something and then again, we may not."

"I'll do what you ask," he said, curious, but willing to wait and trust her to do what she could.

In her heart Loramie was praying, "Lord, don't let me make a mistake, but just save Bill, please!"

She went by the hospital on her way home, but Bill had been given a sedative and was sleeping. She realized, as she looked down upon his pale face, that he didn't yet know the wonderful experience that had come to her in that she had received salvation. There was now no barrier between them as far as spiritual matters were concerned. She remembered how disturbed he had been when he had to explain that passage warning believers not to be unequally yoked with unbelievers and how angry it had made her. Now, if he still wanted her, he wouldn't have to hesitate. She prayed as she stood there, that at least Bill might get well enough to give her the chance of telling him what had happened to her.

When she returned home, she took the little link out of her purse and laid it on the bed before her as she knelt. She prayed that God would guide her as to how to use this little trophy that she had found.

At dinner, everyone seemed in gay spirits, especially Darnell. He was now secure in having his rights to the trapping lands. It only remained for the parish officials to issue the announcement to the trappers and to see that the law was obeyed. If he anticipated any trouble, he showed no signs of worry about it. Loramie surmised that this was because he was depending upon the law to protect him from violence.

Her father seemed in better spirits and now, when she met his eye, she could give him a smile, for her heart held peace within.

"I suppose Fenner will be arrested as soon as he's able to be released from the hospital," Darnell remarked. "When that happens, perhaps these trappers will believe that he's failed them."

"You can't blame him for trying, can you?" she asked sweetly.

"No, I can't, but he was a fool to think he could get away with that crazy scheme," he replied.

"The other day I read in my Bible a passage that says, 'Be sure your sin will find you out.' I'm sure that those words are true."

Darnell gave her a smirk. "When have you taken to reading the Bible? Or believing it? I thought all intelligent people knew that it's just a book of folklore and Jewish fables."

"Then I'm not at all intelligent," she replied gravely, "for I believe that the Bible is the Word of God and that every word in it has come from God and that it was written for our warning and instruction."

His eyes widened in surprise but he didn't answer.

After dinner, as usual, they all sat out front in the late afternoon. The sun was low in the sky and clouds were banked beneath it as it shot forth its golden arrows, tinting them with rich colors, pink and lavender and blue. It seemed to Loramie that that sun was like the eye of God and that it was looking at her with approval.

While they were talking and Darnell, as usual, was telling some joke, illustrating it with a wave of his hands, she stopped him.

"Why, Mr. Darnell," she said, interrupting him, "Your beautiful watchband has been broken. How on earth did you do that?"

The watchband was an unusual one, formed of links richly chased so that they shone in the light as if they were encrusted with diamonds.

He gave a start of surprise and held out his arm, while he looked at the place where there were a couple of links missing.

"I have no idea how it happened," he said as he gave her a grave look. "I must see if I can have a duplicate made of those links. This is a gift from my father."

"I imagine it will be hard to duplicate those links except by an expert jeweler. But I'm sure that someone in New Orleans can do it."

"I'll look into it," he said.

"That reminds me that I think I found one of the missing links," she said. She went into the hall and brought out her purse. "It was so pretty that I picked it up when I found it a little while ago. I thought at first when I saw it lying there in a crack, that it was a little diamond. It looks exactly like yours. It must be one of yours."

She gave him an innocent look as she held the link out to him. He took it reluctantly and held it against the others.

"Why, it does match," he exclaimed. "I can have this to give the jeweler a model to copy from. Where did you find it?" he asked, deceived by her friendly manner and smile.

"I found it in the shack where I was taken when I was kidnapped," she announced gravely. "Can you explain how it got there?"

He stared at her with wide eyes, speechless, while he held the link in his hand and looked stupidly at it.

"What does this mean?" cried Herndon harshly. "How could that thing be found there if you were not there? Can you tell me why?"

Loramie interrupted him as Darnell remained silent, too stunned to think of anything to say.

"I can tell you why, Dad," she said, while her accusing gaze rested upon Darnell. "It was there because Mr. Darnell was there. There is no other explanation. He must have gone there with the man he paid to kidnap me. He is the guilty one and not Bill. I shall be only too glad to appear in court as a witness against him."

"You can't prove a thing!" Darnell cried. His face was white and he knew that his words held no conviction. "It's my word against hers. And I don't even know where that shack is."

"I think her word will stand against yours," Herndon told him.

"I have a witness to the fact that I found this in that shack," she said.

"I shall have you arrested for the crime you were so anxious to pin on another. Why did you attempt such a foolish thing?" Herndon asked.

"I have nothing to say until I've seen my lawyer," Darnell replied defiantly.

"You'd better get a good one," Herndon advised. "In

the meantime, don't try to leave town, for I shall see that you don't."

"I'll be leaving here, since I'm no longer welcome," he said. "I'll get a room in the city until I begin operations here."

"You'll stay right here in town," Herndon told him. "These trappers will be pretty good watchdogs when I pass the word on to them to keep an eye on you. When they know the truth about this affair, your life won't be worth a fig if you try to leave town until this thing is settled."

Darnell went to his room and slammed the door.

CHAPTER 23

LORAMIE KNELT beside her bed before she went to sleep and thanked the Lord for what had happened. She prayed that Darnell would be proven guilty if he really was guilty, and she was sure now that he was.

She remembered the way her guard had acted when he saw that it was Bill whom she had shot. There was terror in his voice and he had gotten away as fast as he could when he had deposited Bill in the back of the car.

Darnell came down before breakfast time with his bags packed.

"I'll take you to the hotel," Herndon told him, "and I warn you that you will be watched day and night. If you attempt to leave, you will run into trouble."

He drove Darnell to the small building that was dignified by being called a hotel, then he spoke to a few trappers who were nearby at a store across the street. When Herndon told them that he was sure he had proof that it was Darnell who had kidnapped Loramie and not Bill, they became excited and angry. He asked them not to stir up any trouble until he had seen the sheriff and had Darnell taken into custody.

After breakfast he went to town to see his lawyer.

Loramie went to the hospital as soon as her father and Darnell had left. She planned to stay there until Bill should be awake. When she went into his room he was just waking up. The nurse told her that he was rational and that he had been asking for her. As she approached the bed, Bill gave her an adoring look. She knelt beside the bed and gave him a smile.

"I'll never forgive myself for what I did to you," she murmured. "I thought you were the one whom the guard said was coming to take me where it would be harder to find me. I never meant to shoot, but my finger pulled the trigger by accident, because I was so frightened. Please forgive me."

"I wanted to tell you about Yvonne, but you wouldn't even let me see you when I came to the house," he said in a weak voice. "I'm sorry you didn't understand. You must think me a terrible person."

His grave look tore at her heart.

"I did for a while," she admitted. "I thought you were the worst kind of hypocrite and I wished that I could hate you, but I couldn't. I even threw my Bible across the room, for I didn't believe a word in it when I thought you weren't living up to what you professed. Then I was so shocked at what I had done. I picked it up and asked God to forgive me. Later on I saw a passage that reminded me of some of the things you had taught me and I got down on my knees right then and asked the Lord to forgive me and to save my poor sinful soul."

"Thank You, Lord," Bill murmured as he closed his eyes while tears trickled down his pale face.

"Then you'll let me explain about Yvonne?" he asked. "I know it looked terrible and I heard what she told you, but I can explain, if you'll only believe me."

"There's no need to explain," she told him. "Mr. Borsage told me all about her. I feel so sorry for the poor little thing. She was standing on the edge of the bayou as we went past the tower on our way to that shack. She was looking for you, for she thought maybe I had taken you away. She doesn't know that you're here, because Mr. Borsage said she might come looking for you and get lost."

"I'm so glad that you knew without having me explain," he said with a sigh. "Why were you and Borsage going to the shack?"

"I wanted to see if there was anything that might give us a clue as to who kidnapped me. The man who held me prisoner said it was you who did it. I couldn't believe him, but he made it seem so plausible. I did find something that may prove that Mr. Darnell did it, not you."

She told him the whole story while he listened with growing amazement.

"I suppose he was trying to destroy whatever chance I might have to help the trappers. He didn't expect me to return so soon."

"He's being held prisoner at the hotel until Dad can have him arrested and put on trial. The only evidence we have is that little link and as Mr. Darnell said, it would be my word against his. I did show the link to Mr. Borsage, but of course they might prove that his evidence was only hearsay, for he didn't see me find the link."

"I think I have enough evidence to prove that he was a fraud and that he didn't really want to do any trapping. He was looking for something more valuable than nutria fur."

"What is it?" she asked.

The nurse felt that Bill was too weak to talk any longer and she advised Loramie to let him take his sleeping pill and rest for a while. Loramie left after promising to come back later. She was curious and anxious to know what Bill had against Darnell, and she could scarcely wait until time to return to the hospital.

During lunch her mother was quite talkative and Loramie smiled at her change of attitude toward Bill.

"I'm so glad that Mr. Fenner will be proved to be innocent of that terrible crime," she said. "He seemed such a nice young man. I'm glad he's getting well. I was so wrong about Mr. Darnell. He certainly had all of us deceived. To think how he abused our friendship and your father's interest in his work. I hope he gets what he deserves."

"I'm glad you changed your mind about Bill," Loramie

remarked with a sly little smile, "because one day he may be your son-in-law."

Her mother stared at her wide-eyed for a moment and the pleased expression faded from her face.

"My son-in-law!" she cried. "I never thought you'd go that far."

"There was a barrier between us and now that has been removed and there is nothing to keep me from becoming his wife, if he still wants me. Bill's time is up here and his health has been restored, so I suppose he will go back home and continue his law practice or go into whatever service the Lord may lead him. Perhaps I shall go back with him. I hope so."

"You know your own heart, Loramie," her mother said gravely. "I suppose as a lawyer's wife, you could be happy."

She had difficulty trying to adjust herself to this situation.

"I'd be happy beyond words, just to be his wife, if he was always only a tower watcher," Loramie replied. "He's a Christian and that's all that matters for both of us."

Before Loramie left for the hospital, Mr. Borsage came. He was quite excited and the words tumbled from him so fast that Loramie couldn't understand what he was trying to say.

"They got him! They got him!" he cried. "Now Bill won't have to worry about any trial. The fellow who kidnapped you was caught and he confessed when he was afraid they would lynch him if he didn't tell the truth."

He told her the whole story. The man who had been hired to kidnap Loramie was a well-known criminal who had been implicated in several robberies in and around Lamare. He had been arrested and put in jail in a nearby town. He had escaped sometime before, but it had been long enough for the search for him to be given up. He had been on his way to a nearby town to commit another robbery that he and his companion had planned before he had been arrested and sent to jail. Both he and his partner now wore beards and they thought that no one in the town would recognize them. While they were there Darnell had met them and had finally made a deal with them to commit the crime he had planned.

Loramie shuddered as she listened to this account. She had been in the hands of ruthless criminals, not just some drifters glad to get a fee. The Lord had certainly delivered her from the danger she had been in.

Her guard had been recognized by one of the trappers who saw him loitering near the bayou. He lost sight of him and forgot about him, but he happened to be in town in the early morning when the fellow was boarding the train. He had the presence of mind to phone the sheriff in the next town where the train was due to stop and the man was taken off the train and held on suspicion.

"They'll keep him there, now that he has confessed, until Darnell's trial. He never did get the money that Darnell promised to pay him and the other fellow, because when everything went wrong, he had to skip out."

The story still had some aspects that she couldn't understand, but she knew that there would be time enough for that later. The thing that was most important was the fact that the fellow had confessed.

Borsage went with her to the hospital. Bill was awake and expecting Loramie.

Borsage told the whole story to Bill.

"That makes me quite happy," Bill said, "but I have good news for you that no one knows about except the two men I took with me when I left town. Darnell wasn't interested in furs. That was only a blind. He was interested in oil. Do you remember Mr. Ranier?"

Borsage nodded. "He's the old fellow who kept saying that he'd found the makings of a gusher. We all thought it was just the silly talk of an old man in his dotage."

"That's what I heard. Some did believe him, but, you remember he died without telling anyone just where he had found the indications of oil. Well, Darnell found out about it from someone when he was down here sometime ago. Evidently whoever told him believed the old man's story. When Darnell came back down here with the story that he was interested in fur trapping, he had a company which was willing to back him while he was trying to locate that spot. He wanted to get the trappers out of the way so that they wouldn't suspect what he was trying to find. He wanted time to locate the place, if possible, and then to get the mineral rights while he was supposed to be doing nutria trapping.

"Just after he came here, I had my suspicions about him, for he wasn't hunting for trapping locations. He was going up and down these streams and going as far inland as he could, searching for signs of that oil. We were looking for it too, though no one but those two knew about it. We finally met a man who had worked for Mr. Ranier who thought he might know the section where Ranier had been working when he claimed to have found oil deposits in the marsh. Even after Darnell came, we kept up the search and finally found the spot. It was on Ranier's land and not on state owned lands. So I went to the city and obtained the mineral rights from Ranier's heirs, two daughters, who were happy to let us have it on a royalty basis."

He turned to Loramie. "That's where I was when I left town and was supposed to be gone longer than I was. Darnell had his spies watching my departure and they made a mistake when they thought I was going further than I did. That day when Darnell saw me go into the record office, I was going there to look over the property lines and then I had the rights recorded. His little scheme to discredit me was a lot of trouble for nothing. I can't imagine what he thought he could do to help himself by getting me out of the picture. I think his hatred of me must have warped his brain."

"Then we'll keep our trapping rights," Borsage said in relieved tones.

"You not only won't have to worry about those trapping rights, but if that oil indication proves to be what I hope it does, you won't need those traps any longer. Those mineral rights are in the name of you trappers. And it is all legally recorded. You'll have so many of the things you've always wanted and never hoped to have."

"And all because of you!" Borsage exclaimed as he took Bill's hand in his big rough one. There were tears in his eyes as he held it and thanked Bill over and over again.

"But how did you happen to be there when I shot you?" Loramie asked.

"When I got back, one of the men said you were missing. They had found out about your being kidnapped. I don't know how they did it, but perhaps we'll know when this mess is all cleared up. At any rate I started looking for you. I knew that that shack would be a likely spot for them to take you, at least for a temporary hiding place, so I went there. I didn't know, of course, that I was being charged with the kidnapping. Darnell had done his best to put suspicion on me, I can see that now. What he wanted was to get me out of the picture for a while, to give him more time to look for that oil. He never dreamed that he would be suspected and if it hadn't been for that little link and for the keen eyes and prompt action of the trappers, he might have gone scot free. I can see the hand of God in it all," he added reverently.

"I know that it was His hand," she agreed.

When Borsage had left to tell the good news to his friends, Bill turned to Loramie.

"There's something that I want to say again, that I said once before," he said in low tones, with a look that made her heart beat with rapture.

She put her finger on his lips. She didn't want him to say what she thought he was going to say, while there was a nurse standing by with curiosity written upon her face.

"Don't say it now," she said. "We'll talk about that later. As soon as you're well enough, we want you to come home and stay with us while you get your strength back. It's the least we can do for you after what I did to you."

"Just as you say. It will always be that way with me," he added with a glowing smile.

As she left the hospital, there was a smile upon her lips and she sang a little song as she rode home. God was in His heaven and all was right with her world.

CHAPTER 24

LORAMIE HADN'T ASKED her mother if it would be all right for Bill to come home to be with them until he could recuperate, but she felt that her mother couldn't fail to agree. She was pleased and thankful when her mother assured her that he would be welcome.

Before Bill was able to be moved from the hospital, Darnell was brought to trial and the case was soon disposed of. Because of the evidence of the link that Loramie had found, and because of the man who had confessed, Darnell was given a stiff sentence. The two others who were implicated were also given sentences that met the crime. Darnell admitted that he wanted to destroy Bill's influence with the trappers as well as to keep him out of the picture for a time, until he could possibly locate that oil deposit. He had to admit that it was a foolish senseless scheme and that it was doomed to defeat from the start. He didn't admit that his hatred and jealousy of Bill had blinded his thinking when he attempted the whole thing.

Loramie couldn't help but feel sorry for him when he was taken out of the court room to prison, for he looked so utterly broken. All of his arrogance and self-assurance had vanished and he looked just what he was, a beaten man. When she remembered what he had tried to do to Bill and that it was because of this that Bill had almost been killed, her sympathy and pity waned.

Bill was happy and grateful for being allowed to recuperate in the Herndon home.

"This is like heaven compared to that stuffy little room I would have had to go to, if you hadn't been kind enough to have me here," he told Mrs. Herndon. "I would have had to stay in the hospital until I could take care of myself and I was getting pretty tired of that place. I shall tell my parents what you have done for me and I know that they will write and thank you for your kindness."

"We're glad to have you," she assured Bill.

She cast a glance a Loramie's glowing face and she knew that she had just as well accept the fact that this good-looking young man might be her son-in-law after all. Since Darnell's treachery had been revealed, she knew what a mistake she had made when she had tried to persuade Loramie to accept his attentions. If Loramie had taken her advice and had fallen in love with that rascal, she would now have a broken heart and she would have no one to blame but herself.

Loramie remained after her mother had left and she smoothed Bill's pillow and asked him if there was anything that she could do to make him more comfortable.

"Nothing except to have you sit by my side and talk to me," he told her.

"I think you had better rest until lunch time," she advised. "I'll come up after you eat and stay with you a little while, but remember, the doctor said you had to be careful and not tax your strength. Your heart still might feel the effect of that operation. Dr. Higbee told me that he had never been quite so nervous in all the operations he has performed, even in heart operations. If he had made just one slip of a fraction of an inch, it might have been the end for you."

"God knew that I had so much to live for that I'm sure He wanted me to live a while longer. Won't you let me tell you what I have in my heart?" he asked. "I do want to tell you, so very much. All through my delirium I was trying to tell you, but something kept holding me back."

"Let's not talk about it until you're well enough for us to sit in the swing together and there is a beautiful moon looking down upon us," she said with a twinkle in her eye. "It's just a notion of mine. You may call it a silly, romantic one, if you want to, but that's the way I'd like to have it."

"Just as you say," he repeated. "Like I said, that will be it from now on."

Mr. Herndon did his utmost to make Bill realize that they were sorry that they had misjudged him and that he was welcome to remain with them as long as he wanted to.

"As soon as I'm well enough, I want to finish the work I started about that oil lease," Bill told him. "From what I've learned from a geologist, there are indications of a good flow of oil. Then I want to go home and set the hearts of my parents at rest about me. My time is up here and I shall be getting back into my law practice until I'm sure that the Lord has something else for me in life."

The days flew swiftly by until Bill was at last able to come downstairs to his meals. He knew that in just a few days he would be strong enough to leave and be on his own again. He was anxious to do that, yet he hated even a short separation from Loramie.

She had been with him as much as she thought best for him. Occasionally she read to him from her Bible and she had the joy of listening to him explain the best he could, the portions she did not understand.

She resolutely refused to engage in any intimate conversation and though he was impatient, he yielded to her desire and longed for the time when he could tell her all that was in his heart.

A few evenings after he was able to get downstairs, they all sat out on the porch after dinner. After a time, the older ones left Loramie and Bill to themselves.

Both parents felt that they knew what was coming and they admitted to each other that they were glad, after all, that it was Bill and were glad that Loramie hadn't fallen in love with Darnell.

When they were alone, Bill turned to Loramie. "There is a beautiful moon out there looking down upon us. Would my lady accept an invitation to sit in the swing beside me? There is something that I would like very much to tell her."

"I accept your invitation, sir," she replied, falling into his mood while she came and sat beside him. "Would you mind telling me what is so important?"

Bill held out his arms and she let him take her into their fold. He bent his head and kissed her gently, then held her close while their hearts throbbed in unison.

"As if you didn't know what I've already told you. I've wanted to tell you what I was once afraid you would never let me say again, how much I love you. I thought Yvonne had killed whatever love you might have had for me."

"I thought she had," Loramie murmured with her head on his breast, "but I found, even when I thought you had kidnapped me, that nothing could wipe that out of my heart."

"I told you once that I had hoped to make you my wife. I hoped to, but I felt that I shouldn't. Before I left, however, I couldn't help but tell you how I felt."

"I understand. You felt you couldn't because I wasn't a believer. I felt angry and resentful when you first explained that to me, even though I saw it in the Word."

"But now the Lord has removed that barrier. I love you, my darling, more than words can tell, even more than my life, and I want you for my wife if you will have me. Will you marry me, Miss Herndon? I would feel honored to have you for my bride."

She laughed and put her arms around his neck while their lips met in a clinging kiss.

"I would consider it an honor to be your bride, Mr. Fenner, and to be your wife as long as life lasts." She uttered a deep sigh. "I've waited so long to hear those words. How I've prayed and waited for them!"

"And yet you put me off all this time," he reproved.

"I wanted you out here where you could hold me in your

arms like you are doing now. Isn't this a much better way?''

"Just as you say," he said playfully. "I repeat, it shall always be that way — until the end."

"There won't be any end," she asserted, "for I shall love you throughout all eternity."

There was silence for a long time while the moon looked down benignly upon them.

They were married in the little church in Lamare. It was Loramie's wish, for there all the trappers could be present and they were there, every one of them, crowding the little church to the fullest. Bill's parents came down for the wedding. They fell in love with Loramie and were so happy for their son and proud of the work he had done there.

Bill had completed his business with the company who was to drill for the oil and he was happy with their conviction that this well would produce a gusher. It meant so much to the trappers who had trusted him so completely.

They left after the reception. The Herndons would soon be leaving for their home in New Orleans.

There were tears in the eyes of Loramie's parents as they told the happy couple good-by, but they had known that they would have to give up their child to someone and they were glad now that it was Bill.

When Bill and Loramie were aboard the plane that was to take them on their honeymoon, Bill turned to his lovely bride and whispered, "Happy, darling?"

"Happy!" she cried. "If I were any happier, I couldn't stand it."

"God grant that I shall always be able to keep you as happy as you are now," he said tenderly.

"God grant that we shall both always be as happy and as much in love as we are now," she whispered.

He bent over and kissed her, while an elderly lady across the aisle looked on with a smile of approval.